feeding

AT NINE

feeding
AT NINE

R.P. MacIntyre

thistledown press

Library and Archives Canada Cataloguing in Publication

MacIntyre, R. P. (Roderick Peter), 1947-
Feeding at nine / R.P. MacIntyre.

ISBN 1-897235-15-1

I. Title.

PS8575.I67F43 2006   jC813'.54   C2006-903737-X

Cover photograph ©Reg Charity/CORBIS
Cover and book design by Jackie Forrie
Typeset by Thistledown Press
Printed and bound in Canada by Marquis Book Printing Inc.

Thistledown Press Ltd.
633 Main Street
Saskatoon, Saskatchewan, S7H 0J8
www.thistledownpress.com

Thistledown Press gratefully acknowledges the financial assistance of the Canada Council for the Arts, the Saskatchewan Arts Board, and the Government of Canada through the Book Publishing Industry Development Program for its publishing program.

Canadian Patrimoine
Heritage canadien

Canada Council   Conseil des Arts
for the Arts   du Canada

CONTENTS

FOREWORD

It never ceases to amaze me how the bits and pieces of past conjecture (what if?) and sheer conjuring come together to make a story. And it never turns out quite the way you expect.

Nevertheless, in this collection there seems to be two distinct epistemologies: one assumes a kind of innocence in which the stakes, although apparently high for the young protagonists, are not a matter of life and death; the second presumes depths that we encounter after the "age of innocence" in which a harder edge more readily leaves it mark.

The overall theme centres around events or situations that are speculative or unexplained. Sometimes the situations are paranormal; sometimes they are "everyday". They leave us wondering at it all. We would not make a meal on the answers. Perhaps we will snack on the questions.

Rod MacIntyre, 2006
Candle Lake and La Ronge, Saskatchewan.

COLM

I must tell somebody this. I will tell you. You are the mythical audience I create in my mind. The patient ever-interested audience. You're a small audience though. Maybe an audience of one. A female audience. Sympathetic. Interested. Probably beautiful too, not distractingly so — guys don't go slack-jawed when you pass, but you're okay. I think you have red hair. Your name is Tess.

I'm Colm, Tess. I'll listen to you too. As soon as you have something to say.

I'm at Uncle Larry's cabin.

Mail only comes here three days a week, and it's a three kilometre hike to the Kroeker Lake Post Office. True, I can drive most of it, but Calvin (my car with a unique and independent imagination) complains mightily about the lousy road. It's actually better now that snow has fallen and filled some of the holes. I have a good fire going and hauled the water in from a hole I chopped in the lake ice so I can relax now, and tell you everything.

One of the few things that Uncle Larry salvaged from his former life as a dentist is this cabin. It's in one of the little subdivisions that surround Kroeker Lake (pronounced Kray-ker) and sits in a cluster of trees a few dozen metres from the south shore of the lake itself. The prevailing wind is from the north, so it collects all its strength, sweeps across the lake ice and drives the frost right through the walls. It's pretty though — blue-blowing snow in that eerie half-light we have at 5:00 PM. I live in my coat, even though I got electricity. I keep blowing breakers trying to avoid becoming an ice cube. The fire's roaring, but I think most of the heat's going straight up the chimney.

Notice I'm putting off telling you why I'm here. Clever of me, huh.

I got kicked out of home. The reason I got kicked out of home was because I got kicked out of school — again. And this time, it wasn't even my fault.

Well, maybe a bit.

It was Calvin. A combination of Calvin and my dad.

Winter set in early this year on the prairies — October and we're already under a foot of snow. Calvin wouldn't start four days in a row, and so I missed my first class all four days. If you skip four classes in a week, you get suspended for a day. That's the rule at Evelyn Weekes Comprehensive. There's no such thing as excuses. (Evelyn Weekes must be quite the old gal. They named a school after her, and she's still alive! Scary. The reason I know she's still alive is because they introduced her at assembly a couple of months ago. Well, she was alive then. Maybe she's dead now. Why am I telling you this?)

Now, I don't care if I get suspended for a day — I don't care if I'm suspended for a week, but my dad does. I was on probation according to him, "One more suspension and you're OUT, Smartass." So we had this big argument, if he'd have let me park in the garage, then my car would have started and I wouldn't have been late for anything.

Maybe his making me park on the street was a plot to get me out of the house. If it was, it worked. My actual leaving was sort of interesting though. My mom disappeared somewhere. She was nowhere to be seen, but my weird little sister helped me pack the few things I took with me. She didn't do it in an

I'm-glad-to-see-you-go way, but was actually trying to be helpful. It was a kind of surprise. Dad sat and read a newspaper — he gets three; it's a lot of work keeping up with the important news of the world, and gives him something to hide behind.

I admit I've been guilty of pretty well everything over the past couple of years. I admit to giving Gloria Sawanko the finger (she called me a dildo) and shooting mustard at Jennifer Greer (she shot ketchup at me); I admit to asking Mr. Lasko what he did with the metre stick besides point with it (he could have put out my eye, he was that close); I admit to bringing booze into school (once — it was an orange, shot with vodka); I admit to swinging David Charpentier by his heels from the school steps (he called my little sister "Sue LaDo" and he was not referring to her hair) and I admit to calling Mr. Roberts a "punctilious troglodyte asshole" (he is — he called me "supercilious" and "neoteric." Two can play the name-calling game). I was just trying to argue my case about my car not starting.

Anyway, coming late four days, and being kicked out of everything for it seems like overkill to me.

The hell with them and the carpet they rode in on. I'm fine. No one's going to bug me here. I cashed a thousand dollar bond my grandma gave me. It's from an account she set up for me a long time ago and neglected to lock me out. I knew it was for a "rainy day" and God, is it pouring now — well, snowing. Aside from raiding 500 bucks from it for Calvin (for which I do feel somewhat guilty, but only because it's been such a lousy investment) I've saved it for just this sort of emergency.

It's not going to last forever though.

Nothing lasts forever, not even this cold, right?

I must tell you about the coyote.

I saw him on the way back to the cabin today. Not too far from here. He crossed the road, stepped a few paces into the woods, then stopped, turned and watched me pass. Coyotes

NEVER do that. I thought briefly of slowing or stopping, but smiled instead. He was beautiful too — a thick, rich coat — a blue-flecked silver roan, with a white belly.

The thing about it is I saw him in the city just before I left. I swear it's the same one and that he's followed me here.

"Not bloody likely," I hear you say (in my mind's ear you have an accent probably east coast to go with the hair — but of course I don't have an accent at all [ha, ha,] or what I have is as flat as a cow pie). Okay, so you're right. How would he travel 300 kilometres north from there? But he sure looks the same, and the way he looks at me. It's as though he's waiting for me to do something. The question is, what?

For instance, a small stream that feeds the lake (and from which I get my water) enters at a bay near Uncle Larry's. A raft is anchored in the bay, frozen now into the ice. In summer, it's a diving platform where I spent many happy hours when I was eleven or twelve, back when my parents were still talking to Uncle Larry.

The raft was a magic place then, a dream-feeder. You could lie on its deck, listen to the lapping water and watch the clouds race by. It floated outside time. And now it sits locked in ice. Someone forgot to free it from its mooring and set it ashore where it spends most winters. Maybe the ice came unexpectedly early and caught whoever's in charge off guard.

But that's not what I want to tell you. I want to tell you about the coyote. I saw him this very morning standing on the raft. He looked as though he had just risen from his haunches. He looked a bit stiff, standing. He cast a glance my way then trotted ashore and disappeared into the low tangle of young spruce.

I imagine him laying on the raft, dreaming.

What do coyotes dream?

They do not dream of Mr. Roberts the troglodyte, or my dad the Smartass rearer. They do dream though. Science has proven that. They twitch. They moan. They have REM.

They probably dream of eating or hunting. Or maybe of being hunted.

I've got a good fire going; the wind has calmed, and the northern lights are splashing above. I myself will dream now. What will I dream? Maybe of you. What do you dream?

Another day, another dollar — except there is no dollar. And really, not much of a day either. There's a steady grey frost lifting off the lake and landing right inside my bones. I swear it's warmer outside. I'm running out of fuel. I'm going to have to go into the woods and start chopping. The exercise will be good for me. It'll keep me warm. This afternoon.

Notice I'm writing little short choppy sentences? It's the equivalent of stomping my feet. Stomping my brain. To keep the blood flowing there. No, this is not nuts. It's a perfectly normal way of staying alive.

An added reason Uncle Larry is on the outs with my mom and dad — aside from his questionable judgment a few years ago — is that he's going with a Cree woman. She is the sister to a guy he became friends with in prison. Her name is Elaine. She has ink black eyes and the same smile the coyote gave me the other day, like she can see things I can't — and thinks that's funny. I hope it is funny because I like her quite a lot.

My parents though, do not. They could probably forgive Uncle Larry for dealing prescription drugs, but they could never forgive him for going out with an "Indian." Racist pigs.

I hope the two of them come out here soon and bring some dry wood!

I wish my dad could see the light. But no, he's like some kind of comic book evil scientist — except he's for real. He's so smart. He reminds me of me. God, I hope I don't "grow up" to be like that. The armchair psychologist sitting on my left brain is saying, "Yes, and that's probably why you got yourself kicked out of school."

Probably.

You pay a price trying to get what you don't want.
And THAT sounds like a bad line from a country song.

It is pretty dismal out here when it's really cold and there's a wind. I have to go out every morning and chop enough wood to keep me going for the day. Occasionally, I chop enough for two days. That usually takes care of my mornings. I have a radio and a TV. The radio comes in pretty much filled with static and the TV gets one snowy CBC station. When I get tired of listening to the static and watching the snow on TV, I turn everything off and listen to the wind and watch the snow out the window. Nothing much changes.

After I've stoked the fire, I hike over to the Stones Throw Restaurant (Garage, Confectionery, Post Office, Liquor Board Store and Gas Bar) sit in a window booth and have a coffee (three milks, four sugars — two refills). I take out my notebook and write to you, Tess. It's actually more of a prop, since I don't generally get much down on paper. But it looks good.

Gladys is the woman who works there all the time. She runs the Post Office and the restaurant. You've got to understand that this restaurant consists of a counter six feet long with three stools at it, and three booths along the front window. Sometimes there are a couple of guys in skidoo suits sitting at the counter flirting with Gladys.

She'd be my mother's age and she likes to tease me. "The Writer" she calls me. "Oh, and how's The Writer today?" "Whatcha writin' about today? You writin' about me?" "I bet you're writin' some girl somewhere." I don't correct her. She knows I'm not because I don't mail anything. "Hey, watch what you're saying or he'll put it in his book," she'll say if there's someone there, and so on. I like her though. You can tell she's had a hard life. Her eyes look like they've seen through a lot of dark time, and she's jumpy and jerky, like maybe she's done a lot of drugs or something. Maybe she's just really nervous. But she's nice to me. I try to be nice back.

Anyway, she's about the only human being I talk to here. Her and Ron. Ron is Glady's brother who's in his early sixties I'd guess, and runs the garage part of the Stone's Throw. They have kind of adopted me lately.

At any rate, Ron's one of those guys who is always doing something involving grease or metal or welding torches, except when he's fishing. Gladys says he used to be a drinker but he's on the wagon now, and has been for thirteen years. I'd say he's pretty well got it licked, but he's very into AA and holds meetings in the church hall every week. Thursdays.

There are two reasons I tell you this: one, Ron has built a fish hut on metal skids; two, people use fish huts to get away from their wives and do a lot of drinking. I don't know if you're familiar with ice fishing, but it's a common practice here. After the ice has frozen hard (and it's certainly done so here) the lake is suddenly dotted with huts and tents, containing a fisher or two, flanked by skidoos and pick-ups. This is especially true on the weekends, but even during the week, a local or two is parked on the ice, huddled in his hut. I shouldn't just say "his" because a lot of women do this too — like Gladys, on Mondays when she closes the café and can get someone to look after the store.

Today Ron asked me if I like to go ice-fishing with him. Not being especially busy I said sure, and before I knew it, I was sitting on the back of his old snowmobile with his hut sliding behind us across the lake. It had already been on the lake amid a veritable village of huts, but the fish weren't biting and he was moving it somewhere else. He had a hunch, he said, the fish were at this new site. I think the real truth was too much drinking was going on inside the neighbouring huts. Outside them, stacks of beer cases spilled empty bottles. Whiskey bottles lay beside them. I just don't think he was comfortable there. I don't blame him.

Anyway, we stopped at a secluded bay. There was nothing around but great expanses of snow-covered ice. The low hills rose off the uninhabited lakeshore and a grey sky hung above. There was not a speck of colour anywhere. No wind.

I helped Ron with the auger which we have trouble starting. After about the thirtieth pull, it starts and we growl a hole in the ice, auger spitting and chewing like some evil hungry thing. We scrape aside the loose ice and slush with a shovel, then pull the hut over top as if to hide our sin. But really, it is to drop our lines through the hole, quick, before it freezes up. Before we freeze up too. It was a chilly ride across the lake on the back of the snowmobile.

Ron doesn't talk a lot. It's like he only owns a few words and doesn't like to waste them in idle conversation. Every now and then, he'll say, "yep," even though no one's asked him to agree with anything. It's one of the words he has extra. But Ron doesn't need to talk. He communicates a lot by just being.

We were sitting inside, all warm and comfy (except for Ron's tobacco smoke) with our lines dangling (you can actually see the lake bottom, and the fish inspecting your bait) when I decided I needed to relieve myself.

"Yep," Ron said before I even began to move for the door.

One of the advantages of being a guy is there aren't many limits on where you can empty your bladder (I'm trying not to be crude here). As long as it's not upwind, and you aren't exposing yourself to charges of public indecency, you're pretty well free. It's actually a cool feeling (both literally and figuratively) to point yourself into the great outdoors and watch the steaming stream arc from your body like the fountain in an Italian village square.

Except when a bear is watching you.

At first I didn't know it was a bear. It was a dark figure near the shore. I thought, "maybe it's a dog, but it doesn't move like a dog, and is too big for a dog, too fat to be a deer, and the wrong colour. I think it's a bear. But what's a bear doing out at this time of year? It can't be a bear!" All these thoughts took place in a lot less time than it took me to zip up my pants.

But yes, it was a bear and it was heading directly in our direction, coming right at us.

I yelled for Ron to come out and see this.

"Yep," he said, and came stumbling out of the hut.

I pointed, and Ron strung together the most words in the few weeks I had known him. And they were a complete waste. He didn't need them.

"Holy shit!" he said. "Bear!"

Now if this were a novel or something, it would be a good place to have a chapter break, just to keep you reading. So I'll insert a little pause here, in case you want to go the bathroom or refill your cup of tea.

This is it:

Freeze-frame — with bear frozen mid-lope in space, white all around.

Okay, ready? Action: bear resumes loping towards us.

Bears can move at a pretty good clip and he's getting closer. It's quite clear we are the bear's destination. The question is, why?

Ron picks up the shovel. He climbs on top of the snowmobile and starts yelling, roaring really.

The bear stops. He's still about a hundred metres away. It looks like the bear is thinking it over. He takes a few paces off to the side, then he turns and starts galloping towards us again.

It's about now I start getting scared. He's not a real big bear, and I'm not even sure he's a he, but he looks like he could do a fair bit of damage if all you've got is a shovel between the three of you. Which is exactly what we have.

When he gets to us, he slows down as if to size up which one of us he's going to go after first. He walks by the hut, swats it and just about tips it over. He's showing off what he could do to us. Ron's got some frozen bait in a small plastic bucket. The bear swats that. It flies ten yards. He starts coming towards me. Ron swings the shovel and smacks the bear across the nose. The bear sits down for a second, stunned.

Ron's got his attention. The bear gets up and starts towards Ron.

I look around for something to hit him with. I pick up the auger. You can't swing an auger, it's too heavy. I pull the chord; it starts first pull and roars to life. I hold the roaring auger over my head as though I am suddenly very big and loud. The bear takes one look, backs off a few paces.

Ron swings the shovel again, bonking him on the head. The bear turns and gallops back the way he came.

Ron and I aren't much interested in fishing any more. And while we pack up the hut and all the fishing gear, the bear paces up and down the shore. He does not go into the woods or wherever it was he came from. He/she is still there when we leave.

Bears are supposed to be hibernating now. Why this one came out to harass us is a mystery. Maybe we disturbed it when we were augering the hole in the ice. (Although I don't see how — we were at least half a klick offshore.) Maybe he was sick. Maybe his internal clock was all screwed up. (I'd be mad too if I woke up in the middle of winter when I thought it should be spring.) Maybe he was hungry and didn't get enough to eat in the fall and his stomach was really grumbling. (There were a lot of forest fires around here last year; food was probably scarce.)

Maybe he was a she. Maybe she was about to give birth.

Still, that wasn't the worst of it. We made it back to the Stone's Throw just after dark. I climbed back in Calvin and pointed it towards the cabin. I was about halfway there when two silver eyes reflected back to me from the middle of the snow-covered road. I slammed on my brakes, but slid right through whatever held those eyes.

When I finally stopped and turned around, my lights shone on whatever it was. As I got closer I could see a small figure dragging itself in the ditch.

It was the coyote.

He was dragging himself backwards towards the woods. I'd broken his front legs. He was whimpering. I wanted to catch him, take him home and heal him. I ran through the snow. I kept stumbling, the drifts were so deep. But he disappeared into the black woods before I got to him.

The next day, as soon as it got light enough, I went back to see if I could find him. I couldn't. I couldn't even find the place where I'd hit him. I was left with the eerie impossible feeling that maybe it hadn't happened. Maybe I'd dreamt it.

But there was a tuft of white stuck in the bumper of my car.

That was my day Tess. I hope you're still there.

My turn to listen. I'll listen hard.

PINK BIKE BLACK

Mister Fogel is skinny and crooked. He might tip over if it gets too windy. His coat flaps like a crow's wings.

He invites me over to play crokinole — a game with little wooden pucks that you flick with your fingers. One person has yellowy-white pucks and the other person has black pucks. The person with the most pucks closest to the middle of the board is the winner. It looks pretty easy but you should just try beat Mister Fogel some time, him and them skinny, crooked fingers.

I ask my mom if we can get a crokinole game and she says why. I tell her Mister Fogel has one. She just looks at me funny and says you can't have everything Hughy. I only have so much money. Maybe some other time.

I'd like to practice so I could beat Mister Fogel.

My sister calls him "Old Fogy Fogel" or "Foggy Fogel" or "Fossil Fogel." I call her "Crazy Caroline" except she's not really crazy. She's just my sister. She calls me "Gooey" because my name is Hughy. Well really it's Hugh but my mom calls me Hughy. So Gooey Hughy rhymes. I don't hate Caroline all the time. But usually I do because she's mean. Her friends are mean too. They're ten and they're girls. I'm eight and I'm a boy. Mister Fogel is way older. He's older than a tree.

So I help him sometimes. In the winter I helped shovel the snow once but I made kind of a mess because I jumped in the snowbank he made and I got out easy but there was snow all over and now in the summer I'm helping him clean out the garage.

Mister Fogel has lots of old things like shovels and rakes without handles, plus a bunch I don't know what half of them are. They are benty and have dents in them. They are rusty and broken. They are tippy and fall easy if you touch them by accident. Like I did. I picked them all back up though and put them in a corner because they get in the way and there's no room for them anywhere else.

That's why I'm helping put stuff into the back of his truck to go to the dump. It's black and just a little truck so I can reach over to get the garbage bags in. The garbage bags are big and soft and hard to lift. They are filled with leaves that fell from trees. They fell from the trees last year when I was seven.

"What makes them fall from the trees?" I ask him.

"I guess they just get tired of hanging on all summer."

"Leaves don't get tired."

"Sure, they get tired and they turn orange and they leave the tree. That's how come they're called leaves because they don't stay — otherwise they'd be called stays. But we don't call them stays we call them leaves." Those lines around his eyes are all turned up like a smile. He's teasing me. He always does that.

Mister Fogel and me go to the dump three times but it hardly looks any different inside the garage except the bags are gone.

"That's all," he says.

"What about all that other stuff?"

"That's all good. You never know when it might come in handy," he says.

It looks like junk to me. But I don't tell him that because maybe he'll want to put some of it in the back of the truck and we'll go to the dump again.

I don't want to go to the dump again. I want to play outside. The sun is warm and shiny so you want to lay on the grass and look up at the clouds making camel shapes. And elephants.

Then I want to go to the park and see how high I can go on the swing. Sometimes it's like you can reach all the way up to the clouds. You have to stand on the swing though; you can't do it sitting. If Jeremy is there we can have a contest to see who can go higher. Then we can play on the slide to see who can go down the fastest. Jeremy likes to put sand down the slide. He says it makes him go faster. I think it just makes your pants dirty and then Mom gets mad, so I don't put sand on the slide when I go down.

Mom doesn't like Jeremy too much. Or his house. She says you stay away from his house. There's always people coming and going there all day and night. I never saw people always coming and going — just sometimes — but I guess Mom did. Like the police I saw there two times. They weren't for Jeremy though. I asked him and he said they were looking for Rick but Rick wasn't there. He said Rick sleeps there sometimes. He's sort of like an uncle but isn't really.

Caroline doesn't like Jeremy too much either because he's always dirty and Caroline's always clean. Sometimes I'm clean, but sometimes I'm dirty too and I like Jeremy because he doesn't care. Even though Jeremy's older than me he's smaller.

Jeremy wears big thick glasses that make his eyes look like onions. He can't always see too good. My sister Crazy Caroline and her friends play tricks on Jeremy and once they took his glasses at the park. Jeremy cried and I told Mom, and Caroline got grounded. If you get grounded you can't go outside to play with your friends and you can't watch cartoons on TV — not even on Saturday. Caroline was so grumpy that Mom let her watch cartoons on Saturday but she still couldn't go outside.

Caroline says if tell on her again I'm in big trouble.

The park is a whole block going one way and two blocks going the other. It's a big rectangle covered in grass and trees.

There are paths between the trees and little hills that are fun to go up and down with your bike. There are sprinklers to go on the grass. They come up like magic out of the ground. There are two buildings at each end of the park with a fence surrounding them like a yard. One of the yards has a real short lawn where old people go bowling. The other has a paddling pool where you can go swimming when there's water in it and the supervisor's there. Just outside the fence beside the paddling pool are swings and a merry-go-round and climbing bars and slides. There's a basketball hoop for the big kids and benches where the moms with babies come to sit and talk. They rock their little babies in the carriage. Sometimes there are bigger babies with those baggy diapers, learning how to walk and they go plonk down in the sand on their butts. They just get up again and their moms chase them before they get too far away. Or they sit there and eat the sand. The babies eat the sand.

I go to the park just about every day. So does Mister Fogel. Except he doesn't go where the other old people go bowling, he comes and sits on the bench with the moms. He doesn't say anything to anyone. He just sits there and sort of smiles. He nods when I say hi to him and smiles louder.

Sometimes the moms have more than one baby. They have one in a carriage and one who is learning to walk. If the one who is learning to walk falls down and cries, his mom runs to him and picks him up. That's when Mister Fogel reaches over and rocks the carriage. Or if the one in the carriage cries while the mom is pushing a little one on the swing, the mom will go to the one in the carriage and maybe Mister Fogel will get up and push that little one on the swing. Except he always asks the mothers first. He doesn't push them very high. He's just helping.

But mostly he sits on the bench and watches us. Or maybe he isn't watching because he's looking right between us somewhere else — like maybe far away past into another day. You can't really tell though.

My sister Caroline got a new bike. She's all happy because it's new and shiny red and she already yelled at me not to even touch it once or I'll get it. But I'll sneak a touch anyway and maybe ride it in the alley when she's not looking. She can't always be the boss. My sister Caroline's getting bigger so she needs a new bike.

So guess what? I get her old one. It works okay but it's a girls' bike. And it's pink. It's bare bum pink. I'm not going to ride a pink girls' bike. I'll ride my old one even though it's too small and I have to scrunch up my knees to pedal. My mom says pink's a nice colour and what's my big problem? If I don't stop my whining, she's going to take them both away. For sure she's giving my old one to my cousin Coglan even though he's too little to ride it yet. She's going to take it there just as soon as she gets a chance.

I tell Mister Fogel I hate my pink girls' bike and he says to bring it over, we'll fix that.

We can't fix it into a boys' bike but we can paint the pink bike black.

In about twenty minutes I have a black bike instead of a pink one. It's still a girls' bike but at least it's not pink and I ride it as soon as it gets dried. I wanted to give my old one to Jeremy because he's smaller than me anyways and he doesn't have a bike. But Mom says Jeremy's mom can buy Jeremy his own bike. I don't think Jeremy's mom has any money or Jeremy would have a bike already.

Me and Jeremy go for a bike ride in the park. I lend him my old one before my mom takes it to Coglan's. It's fun because Jeremy and I never got to do this before together. I can go faster than Jeremy because my bike is bigger. But it doesn't matter. I don't race him all the time because it's not too fair. Jeremy says when he gets a new bike it's going to be bigger and faster than mine. And it's not going to be a girls'. It might be black though. He says it's like Rick's motorcycle. I've seen that motorcycle.

It's got silver flames burning on the black. So I pretend I'm riding a motorcycle.

We go zipping up and down the paths. I see Mister Fogel sitting on the bench and I wave at him but all of a sudden wobble and just about fall. I should keep both hands on the handle bars. The mothers are sitting on the bench too. There are two little diapered kids running with their hands stretched out reaching for nothing but air. We skid around them on the grass. As soon as we pass them, we speed up and go back onto the paths.

There's a turn in the path that goes around a big Christmas tree. You can't see if anyone's coming the other way. I slow down a bit but Jeremy passes me like we're in a race and at the same time my sister Caroline and her friends come around the tree on their bikes. Caroline is leading the way on her new bike because Caroline always leads the way.

Jeremy tries to stop but he crashes like an explosion into Crazy Caroline who falls first — then all her friends fall too — crashing into her or each other, trying to stop. They are like a big junk pile of people and bikes lying on the path. Nobody is hurt. They are just mad because they are all tangled up. Jeremy is crawling on his hands and knees looking for his glasses that got knocked off. They are somewhere under the pile.

"My mom will kill me if they're broken," says Jeremy.

"Are these them?" asks my sister.

"Yeah!" says Jeremy. He's all excited they're not broken.

But Caroline takes them in both hands and breaks them in two. "Here," she says. "That's for breaking my bike."

Jeremy takes the broken glasses and runs. He just runs away. I can't even go with him. I have two bikes to take home.

My sister's really mean. Her bike isn't really broken. It's just scratched a little. I wonder what she's going to tell Mom?

Mom says, "YOU are in trouble mister. Just what happened to those bikes? How can you wreck three bikes in one day?"

"I didn't wreck any bikes. Jeremy did," I say because actually it was Jeremy who bent the wheel on my old one so it is kind of wrecked. But he only scratched Caroline's new one. It's not wrecked.

"Yes, and did Jeremy paint your new one?

"It's not new," I say.

"THE ONE THAT IS NOW BLACK. Who painted it?"

"I did, with Mister Fogel." Mister Fogel painted most of it though. I don't tell my mom that. I don't think it matters.

"I can see that — why?"

"So it wouldn't be pink any more."

"Don't you be smart with me, young man. There was nothing wrong with the colour it was."

She always calls me young man when she doesn't like what I say to her even though it's the truth. So I just look at her. I don't know what else to say. If I tell a lie, she'll get mad. So I'm kind of stuck here, staring at her.

"Tell me why you painted the bike. Painting it like that is like telling people you stole it — especially painting it black."

I didn't know that. It was just the colour that Mister Fogel took off the shelf in his garage. It was in a spray can. He didn't ask if I wanted it black. I probably would have said red. Instead he asked me to spread newspapers on the floor. So I spread newspapers on the floor and he put the bike on them. Then he put tape on the handle bars and some other parts of the bike that he didn't want to turn black. Then he started spraying it. He got lots of black on the newspaper. He said it was a good thing I spread them under the bike. I could tell my mom all that but I don't think it would be the answer that she wants. So I look at her.

"Don't just look at me," she says.

I don't know what else to do.

"Answer me," she says.

Now I'm just afraid that if I open my mouth I'll start crying and I won't be able to talk anyways so I don't say anything again, even though I know my mom is getting mad and it's my fault she's getting mad. I want to go to my room and be by myself. I want to take all the black paint off my sister's girls' bike. I don't care if it's bum pink. I won't ride it anyway. I won't even ride it now that it's black. I want to fix Jeremy's glasses and I want him to have a bike.

"What were you and Jeremy doing racing around the park paths running into people on your bikes?"

"We weren't."

"That's not what your sister says."

"We didn't mean to."

"Yeah, right, 'You didn't mean to.' I'm taking that old bike of yours to your cousin Coglan's this afternoon. And if you don't scrape every bit of that black paint off the other one, I'm taking it too. Now go to your room."

I don't know how I'm supposed to scrape the bike in my room. It would make a mess. I'm not supposed to make a mess in my room.

"Go to your room after you scrape that bike."

Mom gives me an old steak knife and some sandpaper. I scrape. The black paint comes off pretty easy. And so does the pink. Pretty soon it'll be a silver bike with no paint at all. Well not pretty soon. Scraping is hard and slow. At least it won't be a pink bike.

Today I walked home from the park with Mister Fogel. Caroline and one of her friends came racing by us on the sidewalk. She just about knocked Mister Fogel over. He doesn't walk too fast and he's a little bit tippy (or else he wouldn't have fallen into the snowbank last winter.) He just about fell again but I helped him stay up. I yelled at Caroline to watch out. She just kept on going. Mister Fogel asked me how come I wasn't riding my bike. I said I didn't want to. Then he asked me if I wanted to learn cribbage.

Cribbage is a game you play with cards and a board with lots of holes in it. Each player has different colour pegs for their holes. There are 120 holes from the beginning to the end for each player. You move your pegs by adding what goes to fifteen. The first one to finish wins.

"Fifteen two, fifteen four and the rest don't score," says Mister Fogel.

He wins again. He's beat me about five times.

I think it's time to go home.

When I get there, Mom asks where I've been and I tell her Mister Fogel's playing cribbage. She says not to go there anymore. He's not a good influence. I can play cribbage right here at home. Except we don't have a cribbage board. She says I should play with people my own age. There's only girls my own age. There's no boys at all, except for Jeremy. I live in a freaky neighbourhood where all the girls play with Caroline because she's the leader. Jeremy can't go out because he's been grounded for breaking his glasses. "Well then find things to do on your own," Mom says.

There's nothing to do on my own. I can't even lie on my back and look at the clouds. The sky's all gray.

It's going to rain.

Pretty soon the wind comes up and it gets cool then it starts to rain hard. It blows and rains. There is growling in the sky like Rick's motorcycles. Like if he had a bunch of them racing in the clouds. The trees are swaying so hard their branches might break.

Mom is walking back and forth in the living room. She is worried. That's what Mom does when she's worried. She walks back and forth in the living room.

"Where is she?" she says. She doesn't say it to me. More like she says it to the window. The window just shows the storm. It doesn't show where Caroline is and that's why Mom is worrying because Crazy Caroline is out in the storm. She probably doesn't have her raincoat either. "She knows better than that," Mom says to the window again. Secretly I'm kind of glad that Caroline is out in the storm getting wet. It'll teach her right. For being so bossy and hogging the sidewalk. And breaking Jeremy's glasses.

But when it starts to get dark, I start to get worried too. "If she's not home by 8:30, I'm going to call the police," Mom says. She has already called some of Caroline's friends' parents, but she doesn't know all their names and numbers. Neither do I.

Finally at twenty after eight just when Mom is looking at the phone we can see Caroline walking down the street. She looks wet even though the storm has stopped and it's just spits of rain. "Thank God," says Mom and she takes a deep breath. I can't tell if she's going to be happy or mad.

Caroline steps through the door and Mom yells, "Where have you been? Do you realize what time it is? That you've missed supper. I've been worried SICK."

She's mad I guess.

Caroline doesn't get mad back like she usually does. She just opens her mouth and starts crying. Sobbing big sobby sobs. Then she hugs me. Or leans on me while she's snuffling away getting me all wet. I can't figure out why she's hugging me. I never hug her.

When she finally stops sobbing and hugging and Mom has put a towel around her to keep from dripping all over the place. "It's okay. It'll be okay," Mom says. Finally Caroline can talk enough to tell us that she lost her bike. Her brand new bike. Someone stole it. A bike burglar. That's why she was out in the rain in the storm. She was looking for it. But she couldn't find it and she starts sobbing again.

I tell her she can have her old one back even though it's not pink anymore. She just keeps sobbing. Maybe even louder. Mom gives me a hug and says, "That's very sweet Hughy but I think she wants her new bike back."

Not her old one which isn't pink anymore.

It's the next day when there are puddles all over with drowned worms in them. Just millions of them. The robins are happy. This is more worms than they can eat. I almost wish that I was a robin. But then I would have to watch out for cats. Anyway Mom has called the police to report Caroline's stolen bike and they tell her to come on down and have a look at their stolen bike collection. Maybe it's there.

So we go down to the stolen bike place and it's FULL of bikes. There must be a million bikes here — more than worms. Except there's only three picked up in the last day and Caroline's isn't one of them. We go back home.

When we get to our street we see an ambulance and a police car and fire engine outside Mister Fogel's house. All their lights are flashing. Maybe Mister Fogel shot a burglar who was trying to burn down his house and that's why they're all there. Or maybe a burglar shot Mister Fogel. Maybe it was the bike burglar.

"Somebody must have dialed 911," says my mom.

"I'm going to see," I tell her.

"No you're not," she says.

But I do anyway. Mister Fogel is a friend of mine.

"Hugh!" Mom calls. But I keep on walking. "Go with him then," I hear her telling Caroline.

When we get close to Mister Fogel's house a man and a lady are pushing a bed with wheels out of the door and there is someone on the bed. The lady is holding a plastic mask you can see through over the person's face.

"It's Mister Fogel," says Caroline.

I stand on my tip toes and I can see it really is him. I'm suddenly very scared for Mister Fogel. They put him in the ambulance. I get a funny scary feeling inside me like I lost something, maybe like Caroline felt when she lost her bike and I start crying. It makes me so sad that they're taking Mister Fogel away in the ambulance and he has a plastic mask covering his face like he can't breath.

Caroline hugs me. "It's okay. It'll be okay," she says.
This time I hug her back.

It's the next day when I'm on my way to the park that I see
Mister Fogel's garage door open. Somebody should close it. I
don't know if anybody will. Mister Fogel's black truck is there
and all his benty old tools too but something red is shining in
the back of the garage. I go closer to take a better look.

It's Caroline's new bike.

I get all excited and I want to take it home to Caroline right
away. But then I think how come Mister Fogel took Caroline's
bike? He's not a bike burglar. Is he? Then I decide I'm not going
to tell anyone where I found it. I'll say I found it under some
bushes in the park. I don't want people to think that Mister
Fogel is a bike burglar.

Caroline is all happy and she jumps up and down when she
sees her bike. Mom is pretty happy too and she gives me a big
hug. She asks me where I found it and I tell her. But Caroline
says she looked under all the bushes in the park. "Well you must
have missed one," says Mom. "I thought I looked under them
all," says Caroline. But they stop talking about it and pretty
soon Caroline goes out to ride on her bike.

I don't feel like doing anything. I feel pretty sad actually.
Maybe it's a good day to lie on my back and look at the clouds.
That's what I do. I see a rabbit and a dog. And the top half of
a giant.

One day a big man with long skinny legs closed Mister
Fogel's garage door. But first he moved Mr. Fogel's black truck
out onto the street. The big man had trouble folding his legs
all up to get into the little truck. Finally he drove it away.
Another time he was in the yard with a lady. They were looking
around at the house. They put a For Sale sign in the yard. Then
a moving van came and two men moved all the stuff out of
his house and his garage.

I wonder what happened to Mister Fogel but I don't know who to ask.

Jeremy is over being grounded. He has to be careful with his new glasses so sometimes he takes them right off when he sees Caroline and her friends coming. He takes them off when we go swimming in the paddling pool too. He doesn't want them to fall into the water. They would be hard to find.

We play lots in the park. Sometimes I ride my bike but not much because it's no fun riding alone all the time. It's also no fun riding a girls' bike all the time either. It's starting to get some rust on it. It also reminds me of Mister Fogel. I sort of miss him coming to the park every day and sitting on the bench with the mothers watching. I'm also sort of glad he doesn't come to the park because I don't know what I would say to him about stealing my sister's bike. I still haven't told anybody where I really found it, not even Jeremy.

The For Sale sign is gone in front of Mister Fogel's and it looks like someone else is moving in, another man and lady. He's got a beard and is fat. So is she. Fat. They're always burning a barbecue in their front yard. They have a dog that looks like a pit-bull. My mom says stay away from there. I will. I walk on the other side of the street when I pass their house. Their lawn is already brown from what that dog is doing. It must be from all the bones they give him from the barbecue. He's not fat though and he's worn a path around the fence where he runs and barks.

Summer is too short. There's not many days left at the park. Next week school starts again. I'll be in grade three. Jeremy will be in grade four. Crazy Caroline will be in grade five, except she's not as Crazy as she was when summer started. She doesn't call me Gooey as much and she doesn't pick on Jeremy any more. Maybe it's because he's not as small as he used to be. I don't know why she doesn't call me Gooey.

Jeremy and I are playing Secret Alien and our spaceships are the swings where we have little stones in our hands and are bombing Stardasic Warriors which are really little mounds of sand underneath us. I got three hits so far and Jeremy only has two. "You got bigger stones," he says but really they're the same size. I just had more. I have to get out of my spaceship to get more ammo when I see a big tall man pushing a wheelchair towards the bench. I get a funny feeling when I see the tall man because I've seen him before. He was the one who drove away with his legs all folded in Mister Fogel's black truck. I look hard at the man in the wheelchair.

It's Mister Fogel. He looks way older than before. His skin looks like paper that's been folded and unfolded. He's wearing a hat and a coat even though it's warm outside. He's a little bit tilty to one side. There's a skinny package tucked in the chair on the other side.

The tall man parks Mister Fogel beside the bench. He straightens Old Mister Fogel then takes the package from the wheelchair and sets it on the bench next to him. He sits too. I walk very slowly towards Mister Fogel. I don't know why I'm walking towards him because I'm actually kind of scared. I don't know what I would say to him. But it's like an invisible string is pulling me towards him and I go even though I don't want to. Then he sees me and his eyes light up and half his face smiles but the other half stays the same.

Suddenly my sister roars up on her bike. "Mister Fogel!" she says. "Where have you been? We've missed you."

Missed trying to run him over, is what I think. But Mister Fogel continues with his lopsided smile and the tall man answers. "He's been in the hospital. He's been very sick. He had a stroke. He's my dad." All of sudden, in his face I can see how Mister Fogel might have looked when he was younger, even though his son looks too old to be a son.

"Can't he talk anymore?" asks Caroline.

"I'm afraid he can't. He can make some noises and write a little with his left hand."

Mister Fogel nods his head a bit and makes some noises just like the Mister Fogel's tall son said he could. It sounds like, "uh, uh." He makes a small waving motion with his left hand that covers his right hand on his lap. That's to show he can write a little with it I guess.

"He wrote 'Park' this morning," says the Tall Mister Fogel, "and I knew exactly what he was talking about because Dad helped build this park over fifty years ago, didn't you Dad."

He looks at Old Mister Fogel and then keeps on talking to us. "He chopped and he scraped and raked and pulled rocks and he shovelled and planted trees and grass and built the little hills. AND he did the whole thing by hand. Why, he even kept some of those old tools he used here in his garage, didn't you dad," says Tall Mister Fogel. Old Mister Fogel is half-smiling and going, "uh, uh." "The only thing that's changed in fifty years is the trees are taller. So he's always had a special fondness for this park. It gives him great pleasure to see all the children playing in his park."

There are tears starting up in Mister Fogel's eyes. I can tell that I'm never going to ask him about the bike. My sister puts her hand on Mister Fogel's like she's trying to keep him from crying. If she only knew who took her bike. Mister Fogel looks at me. He makes some noises, "Uh, uh," he says. I look away. I walk away.

I go back to the swing. Jeremy is still there. I don't feel like playing Secret Alien anymore. I just want to lie down somewhere and look at the clouds. Or maybe listen to them roar. "Come on," I say to Jeremy.

Jeremy and I are lying on the grass on a little hill looking up at the sky. It is so clear blue, it almost hurts your eyes.

"Know what?" says Jeremy.

"What?" I say.

"I got a secret," says Jeremy.

"Me too," I say.

"You tell me yours and I'll tell you mine," says Jeremy.

I think about this. I don't know if I want to tell Jeremy my secret.

"You tell me your secret first," I say.

"Okay," says Jeremy, "I took Caroline's bike."

"No you didn't," I say.

"Yes I did. And I put it into Mr. Fogel's garage."

"What?" I say and I look at Jeremy to see if he's smirking or just trying to make a joke. But he isn't. I know he's telling the truth.

I get up and I run as fast as I can back to where Mister Fogel was sitting by the bench. But he's not there any more.

Mister Fogel is gone.

When I get home my mom says Caroline brought a package for me from Mister Fogel. I open the package. In it is a cribbage board with a deck of cards.

My mom asks me why I'm crying, what's the matter?

"I don't know," I say.

HANKWOMAN

Although Curley swept classroom floors for a living, he loved these three things most, though not necessarily in this order: the wind on his face, Delta style blues and Hankwoman Baker — master mechanic mother of his daughter.

His bike was British, a 1952 Ariel Square Four 1000 built shortly after they went to the aluminum block. It was a remarkably smooth yet ponderous ride due to the configuration of the pistons which was jargon for, watch out, top-heavy. He was on his way to see his wife when a dog crossed in front of him. He swerved to avoid it and because 22nd Street was not paved in those days, the front wheel dug into the wet gravel.

An odd thing happens to light when you are upside down, near death — it sharpens. Or maybe it just slows.

Sliding on his skull, he could see how each stone of gravel glistened after the recent rain. And the sound . . . Something growled for a second or two. Maybe it was the engine. Maybe it was the bones in his neck or shoulder. Maybe it was the gravel. He was still saddled to the bike, but beneath it. All 463 pounds of motorcycle now rode him in these drawn-out milliseconds. He was going too slow to have been thrown clear. He thought, I'm glad this helmet is holding together.

The only problem was it didn't.

Four days later, Hankwoman and Curley's infant daughter watched as he was lowered into his grave.

If you wanted to make someone comfortable, you would not open the conversation by saying you had lung cancer. No, you would not do that. And if you did, you would want to make amends for it somehow, perhaps with a gift.

Still, the promise was one that you'd expect Ariel to keep — after she found out about her mother's disease. But what, really, would an aspiring choreographer — a failed ballerina — do with an ancient motorcycle she didn't know how to ride?

Henriette Baker was born just after the war. Her father, Henry, owned Baker's garage where she, her parents and four older brothers all worked. The smell and hue of metal and gas was fixed in their pores like smoke. They took on anything with an internal combustion engine — from two-ton trucks to lawnmowers. The Baker garage was an old horse barn with two work-pits and a hoist. It had gained a reputation for honesty and ingenuity — if they couldn't find the part you needed, they made it for you. A metal lathe was mounted on a workbench. Every assortment of tool and die lined the walls and filled metal cabinets which had once glistened fire-engine red but were now caked in grease and those mystery tars from countless cigarettes. All the Bakers smoked. Henriette began when she was ten. But everybody smoked cigarettes back then.

Mr. Baker strained hard to be a respected member of the community. He didn't like that his name had been shortened from Henry to Hank. He wasn't just a grease monkey but could rebore a cylinder wall within a sixty-fourth of an inch, just like Mrs. Baker didn't just keep her hair in curlers but did their books and prepared their neighbours' income tax returns for a small fee. Mr. Baker also joined a service club attached to the

YMCA known as the Y's Men. Their big annual fundraiser was selling Christmas trees. Henriette's mother had belonged to the women's auxiliary of the Y's Men. They were not known as the Y's Women, as one might expect, but the Y's Menettes.

Henriette's brothers were so amused they began calling her Hankette before she started school. By the time she was thirteen, Hankette could lay a bead with an acetylene torch better than most girls her age could apply mascara to their lashes.

There was no room for feminization in Hankette's life. She was too busy tearing down small engines. Over time, her specialty became motorcycles — 50cc dirt bikes or 1200cc cruisers — two stroke or four. It didn't matter to her. She liked the machines and she liked their riders. It was how she met Curley.

Curley was a big man with a big bike. Both were twice her age but not twice her size. Hankette was bigger than two of her brothers and towered over her dad. She was nearly seventeen.

Curley took one look at Hankette and fell in love. He wanted an overhaul — new pistons, sleeves and timing belt. He wanted his tongue to find language, his heart to quiet. When Curley discovered Hankette was a woman, he was ecstatic — for there was a short time during which he was unsure. To remind himself, he dubbed her Hankwoman. It caught on with her brothers as well. Soon everyone called her that. She didn't mind. It was better than Hankette, and way better than Henriette.

However, while she was still Hankette, she was perplexed by Curley's attention. He seemed to want something from her that she didn't know she had. Something besides her deft abilities with a wrench. It seemed he wanted her. She couldn't figure out why till the day she smashed her thumb with a ball peen hammer trying to loose a set of frozen insert bearings, and Curley was at her side with a bag of ice and a wash cloth in seconds flat. He took her hand and touched it with such tenderness that Hankette forgot totally about the pain, looked Curley in the eye and put her good fist into his nose.

That was how it started.

Curley eventually found his voice and it sounded like a steam shovel digging out a gravel pit. He played a flat-top box guitar in open tuning and made up songs like this:

I got a big bike
I got a great big bike
I got a momma too
And momma's mouth is big as you
I got a great big bike and a momma too

We're riding down the highway
Going a hundred and two
Hit one hole say bye-bye blue

Twelve months later, Hankwoman delivered a child, a girl child. She named her Ariel, not after the Shakespearean fairy, but the motorcycles. It was, of course, the Ariel Square Four 1000 that Curley rode avoiding the dog crossing the street. The dog survived. Curley didn't see his daughter's first birthday.

It was difficult enough for Hankwoman to be a single mother but she didn't have any idea how to raise a girl child because she'd never really been one herself. This didn't bother Ariel for a moment. She seemed to know all about it. She wore or wanted to wear the frilliest, pinkest outfits she met. She played with dolls, make-up and pretend-jewelry. She imagined castles and princes and their dashing white steeds. She wanted to be a ballerina. She never went near the garage.

Ariel had a string of daddies. She paid them no attention. They all rode motorcycles. They all rode in and out of Hankwoman's life.

The Baker Garage eventually became Baker Motors, a large company that distributed and serviced heavy equipment like bulldozers, earthmovers and cranes. Hankwoman did not follow her brothers into the business although she kept her share. She ran a small repair shop to service a select clientele and restore exotic, antique bikes.

Ariel studied ballet. At ten, she was invited into a school that trained gifted students for classical dance. She boarded there. Ariel possessed unusual strength, grace and flexibility. However, like her parents, she also possessed size. At fifteen, 173 centimetres and sixty-five kilos, she might make the back of the corps de ballet, but unlikely a principal dancer and certainly never prima ballerina.

Ariel's visits with her mother were quiet events. For starters, they didn't have the same language. Hankwoman did not know the difference between a "pointe tendu" and a "rond de jambe," and Ariel had no concept of compression ratios. It was frustrating to explain the details of what happened at the "barre" because her mother would first imagine her daughter lining up for a drink, before remembering that the barre is the railing that dancers hold onto for warm-up. Likewise, Ariel looked stupidly at her mother's parts catalogues, utterly immune to discussions of the virtues of one supplier over another.

But, like many dancers controlling their weight, Ariel had taken up smoking and this was a comfort to Hankwoman. Although they didn't smoke in the house, they would go into Hankwoman's shop where they shared a blue haze that filtered through their lungs. It was perhaps the only thing between them as thick as their blood.

Although her mother sometimes missed Ariel's recitals — the travel being too awkward or expensive — she had promised to attend her senior choreographic workshop of Les Sylphides, Michel Fokine's *Chopiniana*. It was a major exercise for Ariel because it might become an option in her career plans. She was crushed when Hankwoman did not show up. She phoned and after a brief, unsatisfactory greeting, she went straight to the point. "Why weren't you there?"

There was only silence from the other end of the line.

"Mom, talk to me!"

The silence indicated that something was clearly wrong. Finally, Hankwoman answered. "Can you come home Sweetheart? It wouldn't be right to tell you on the phone."

"What wouldn't be right?"

"To tell you what I have to tell you."

Ariel was on the next bus. She couldn't wait for a plane even though it would have been faster. She wanted to be moving. She needed to feel that she was doing something besides waiting.

She took a cab from the bus depot. Their house was still in the same neighbourhood as the old Baker's garage. She ran to the door and pushed it open.

"Mom! Mom, I'm home!"

There was no answer. She ran up to her mother's room. It was empty. The bed was made. She looked for a note, for some sign of what might have happened. She peered out the window. The light was on in the shop. Above the door, a small sign — Hankwoman's.

Seconds later, Ariel entered. "What are you doing here? I thought you were sick!"

"I didn't say I was sick. I built something for you — restored it, really." And with that, she removed a dust cover from a motorcycle mounted on a work stand.

"What is it?"

"It's an Ariel Square Four 1000, what your father rode."

"An Ariel?"

"Square Four 1000. It's British."

"I'm named after a motorcycle?"

"It's for you."

"I choreographed a dance two days ago. It's Russian. It was for you — but you didn't come."

"I'm sorry." She took a drag of her cigarette.

"Yeah, well I'm sorry too!" With that, Ariel turned to leave. She reached the door before her mother spoke again.

"I had some tests."

Ariel stopped, her hand on the door, turned — "What kind of tests?"

"Tests." Hankwoman approached her daughter, took her hand and placed it on her chest. "Here," she said. "The doctor has given me less than a year — if the treatments don't take."

"Oh, Henriette!" Ariel exclaimed and clutched her mother in a spontaneous burst of compassion, hugging her close.

In her arms, Ariel felt her mother shaking, as though she were sobbing. Ariel held her closer. But the sounds her mother made were not sobs. They were . . . chuckles.

Hankwoman was laughing.

Ariel pushed her mother to arm's length. "What are you laughing at?"

"You called me 'Henriette'," she said, and began again.

In a great release of tension and before she knew it, Ariel stood laughing too. Mother and daughter stood clutched in each other's arms, laughing till tears coursed from their eyes. It was then that Hankwoman made the request.

"You must promise," she said, "to give me a ride on it."

"On what?" asked Ariel, wiping tears from her cheek.

"On the bike!" her mother said indicating the gleaming machine, and erupting into another spasm of laughter.

Ariel croaked, "But I don't know how to ride!"

"You have a good six months to learn," Hankwoman said, leaning now to steady herself, having grown weak from laughter.

"I will, I promise," said Ariel.

Ariel finished off her school term, graduated and began looking for work. Her training would at least get her onto a chorus line. She auditioned for a part in a new musical where her size was actually an advantage. She got the job. In six weeks, she had another.

"I feel fine!" Hankwoman said when Ariel called to tell of her good fortune. "I'm a little tired, that's all. When will you be able to get away?"

"Soon. Maybe next month," Ariel answered.

"That long? I found some old things of your father's I should show you."

Ariel thought she detected a hint of urgency.

Although no mention was made of the promise, it hung on Ariel like a burr in a woolen sock. The more you picked at it, the more it fragmented and the deeper it dug. It was such a silly promise. How was she going to learn to ride a bike? When? Why did she make such a promise?

Still, Ariel visited her mother at the first possible opportunity. She was shocked at how gaunt she had become. A waxy sheen had transposed upon her boyish face. Her wig fit badly. She had penciled in a set of eyebrows. The radiation treatment and chemotherapy were not achieving their intended effect.

The pair walked slowly to Hankwoman's workshop where they could smoke. It was also where she kept a few of Curley's things. Hankwoman held a ready cigarette in one hand and a lighter in the other.

"When are you going to take me for a ride?" She lit the cigarette.

"Do you mean on the bike?"

"What do you think I mean?"

Ariel knew perfectly well that the Ariel 1000 stood collecting dust.

"I'm taking lessons," she lied.

Hankwoman let the subject drop, although she doubted her daughter's words. There wasn't any point in pressing now. It wasn't going to happen, and what did it matter anyway?

They entered the shop. "He made songs you know. Kind of bluesy things," she said blowing blue smoke into the light beaming through the window. She reached into a cupboard and pulled from it a small scrap of paper from a box full of similar scraps.

She read.

She asked me for a piece of paper
She asked me for my pencil
Yes, she asked me for my pencil
And she asked me for my eraser too

But my eraser's all chewed up
She can have my pencil
And all my paper too
But my eraser's all chewed up
Some people get almost everything they want
But all I got's an eraser
And it's all chewed up

"What's it mean?" Ariel asked.

"I think it means you can't change things," said Hankwoman. "He wrote on these little scraps of paper."

Ariel knew he had been school janitor. She wondered if he had pilfered from students' notebooks.

Hankwoman held up the paper. "You want it?"

"Yes, of course," said Ariel.

Instead of handing Ariel the box containing the paper, she handed her the lighter.

"Set fire to it when you're done, okay?"

"Why?"

"Because it's garbage," said Hankwoman.

Three months later, after the funeral, Ariel returned alone to her mother's workshop. The burnt out piston she used as an ashtray was still filled with cigarette butts. The 1952 Ariel Square Four 1000 still stood beneath its cover. She had never found the time to learn to ride, or more correctly, made the time. But really, it was as though her mother knew she was asking for something Ariel would not — perhaps could not — deliver. Why ask? What sort of stupid test was that? And then there were her father's scraps of paper. She had read through and sorted them all — more or less according to neatness and legibility. Many were partially incomprehensible; some totally.

She gathered them all together and placed them on the floor. She set fire to them and watched as the flames danced, performing an allegro of batteries.

She removed the dust cover and mounted the bike. She sat on the firm leather seat and imagined the wind on her face. A song formed its shape within the rhythm of her blood. She felt her mother's warm arms wrap about her waist.

ANNA'S FLOWERS

The winter I was seven, my neighbourhood was devoid of children near my age — except for Anna who lived next door. She had the green eyes of a cat and moved like one too. She liked to wrestle with me in her basement where we had to play because it was too cold outside. She usually named the games and listed their rules since she was more than a year older than me.

Even though Anna was small, she was strong and we were evenly matched at wrestling. We rolled around the dingy rec room carpet trying to pin each other's shoulders to the floor because that's what they did on TV — that was the game. The rules of this game demanded that I take off my shirt because on TV wrestlers didn't wear shirts. However, girls didn't wrestle (on TV) so that rule didn't apply to her. We wrestled till we were tired and sweaty, and then one of us would start giggling. Quickly contagious, the giggles would spill from us like small silver coins, rolling and bouncing off the floor and walls, till finally they quivered and lay still inside us when we would breathe deep again.

She liked to touch my hair because it was wiry and red — so unlike hers, wispy and blonde. We couldn't have been more different. I came from a place where the waves crashed all winter against the shoreline rocks and where sea peas and oyster grass hung their bluish green leaves and pink blossoms. Anna came from a country far away where bombs crashed at night in waves of thunder.

"They make flowers in the sky," she said.

We were both immigrants to this cold, dark prairie city where snow and ice locked us inside our houses — and bodies — the only places we could explore.

One day, while her father slept on the couch and her mother was at work, and before we began wrestling, Anna closed the door to her room.

"Let's have a contest," she said.

"What kind?" I liked contests.

"If I pin you, you have to pull down your pants. If you pin me, I have to pull down mine," she said.

"What if it's a tie?"

"It can't be a tie."

"Then I don't want to play."

"We can pretend it's a tie, then we both have to pull down our pants." Neither of us liked to admit defeat.

"Okay," I said

On the count of three, and without any wrestling at all, we did it. Our pants were around our ankles.

"You have a penis," she said. She was happy about this. "Can I touch it?" Anna asked, holding her finger out. She was going to anyway, I could tell. So I said yes. And she did. It tickled. I wanted to pull my pants back up. Anna didn't have anything to touch. It was just smooth and bare. I didn't know what to say.

"You're supposed to put your penis in here and we can make a baby." She showed me the crease where my penis was supposed to go — except it looked way small and I didn't believe her. I was too scared to make a baby anyway. What would I do with a baby? How could I explain it to my mom? So I said no. And pulled up my pants.

Later, when I told my mom that Anna wanted to make a baby, she didn't let me go there to wrestle any more.

But I liked Anna. I cut a purple flower from a book. I gave it to her on the way home after school because there were no flowers in winter.

"I hate flowers," she said. "I hate you." She kicked the paper flower in the snow.

I saw her occasionally on the street but she would not look at me with her green cat eyes. Then we moved to another part of the city and Anna almost passed from my memory. But once in a while when a cat crossed my path, I would think of Anna and her green eyes.

Life goes on. I finished high school and tell people I dropped out of university, but really I failed — I was having too much fun. I drive cab now and read a lot between trips. I like studying people, reading between their lines, and I indulge my belief that I am somehow protected — distanced — from them by the metal skin of my cab. But it surprises me when my past suddenly appears to remind me of where I've been.

Last week I saw Anna. I hadn't seen her since grade two, but it was her. She pushed a baby carriage on the snow-packed street struggling through the ruts. The baby in the carriage was crying. I wanted to say hi, but she walked right by, looking straight through me as though I were a shadow. She carried a purple bruise around her left eye. I thought of flowers.

INVISIBLE TO DOGS

I've been here thirteen years now and have seen everything Carl has ever done since he was old enough to think for himself — which in Carl's case might have been delayed a couple of years. My wife's a teacher here and she's seen him try to get through school since kindergarten. We talk — I know we're not supposed to but we do — we're normal. How do you not talk about things?

In Carl's mind, I'm likely just another stupid, old-fart cop who's out to get him, but really, I'm just doing my job, maintaining *le droit*. It never ceases to amaze me in my twenty-three years of police work how people swear their innocence — or in Carl's case, his dog's innocence — no matter what.

"He's innocent. He wouldn't do that. You don't have no proof." Carl whined like a chainsaw. But it was clear they were both guilty as sin, him and his dog. You don't wear a look like that if you're innocent, that pee-pool on the floor look. No, you don't do that. That'll get you nowhere. It never does. Bodies are strewn across the entire planet, their life's blood settled like blue lead in a bag, and no one says they did it. No one claims responsibility.

Still, it was nice to see him take a stand. Carl usually just let people think whatever they wanted. And people being people, always thought the worst, and they were usually right. So it was hard to imagine why he should make such a claim this time. But if his dog didn't do it, who did? I don't even want to go there.

The last time Carl got caught for something, it was for stealing a truck. He was still in it so that made things a little simpler. Carl liked things to be simple and needed them that way too. The shortest distance between two points is a straight line, and Carl was not one to go looking for curves. You want something? Take it. You don't want something? Throw it away.

Carl didn't like his name too much — too many curves in it. The sound alone had a curve in it, not to mention the half-looped "c". He would have preferred something straighter, Stan say, or Joe like his uncle. In grade school, Carl had tried to get people to call him Ike for a while, like the American President, but it didn't catch on. There was no reason to call him Ike, other than Carl telling you to, and no one ever listened to Carl. Which was fair enough because Carl never listened to anyone either — certainly not his mom, and he didn't have a dad. Kids like Carl never do.

Carl was two grades behind so he quit school and got a job at Manny's Muffler, Battery and Brakes. Then he moved out of his mom's basement, and got a dog. He called the dog, "Ike." The dog was a dumb as a post — which is to say, it was slightly smarter than Carl. He would take off at night and go chase cars or trucks. Unlike most dogs, Ike knew what do when he caught one. He'd follow the vehicle till it stopped then attack the driver as he (or she) was getting out. He'd go for their feet.

The amazing thing was that Ike was blind. He had eyes the colour of half-boiled egg whites.

It took a while to figure out just whose dog was doing this and identify it, but when I finally did and notified Carl that I was coming to destroy Ike, he said he'd do it himself. And to prove he did it, he came into the office and plunked the dog's carcass on my desk, minus the eyes. "Ravens got 'em," Carl said.

It was a messy kill. His jaw was shot off and a fair amount of his blood wrecked half of last month's traffic reports, not that anyone reads them anyway. When they dried, I filed them like they were. The Ike reports.

I suppose the reason Carl liked the name Ike, aside from it being straight and short is because he thought it was presidential. Presidents had power and Carl had none. Maybe he thought some of that power came with the name. Carl couldn't have remembered that Ike's last name was Eisenhower, a name as curvy as Maryanne Ravenhurst, the girl found lying on the road just north of here by someone walking their dog. She was more dead than alive, like that victim last year mauled by a bear, except she didn't get buried and it wasn't her head chewed off.

∾∾∾

"Aren't you afraid?" I hear this all the time. It's silly what people assume of girls who enjoy being alone. People are afraid or brave, like some people are tall or short, or have other distinctive characteristics. Fear has nothing to do with gender; it's simply an attribute — like Carl Danziger has four toes, and I am invisible to dogs. Which is very handy, because I love running and my normal route takes me down Churchill Drive past a zillion dogs, out onto "the lake trail" north of town, cluttered with hardy outdoorsy types exercising their canines. It doesn't bother me if they're not leashed.

The only thing that makes me feel vaguely uncomfortable is being oggled. I hate it when people stare at me. It gives me the heeby-jeebies. Especially when creeps like Carl Danziger do it. I can feel his eyes crawl on me like baby mice. Ever since grade three when he would follow me home from school, thinking I couldn't see him. But I could. Just like that time I saw his four-toed foot when his socks came off in his too big boots, and he'd hurried to put them back on. I'm grateful he dropped out of school a couple of years ago and no longer lurks in the hallways, limping from locker to locker.

Since this is a northern town, it is filled with dogs and ravens; the dogs come in two sizes: large and extra-large; the ravens, just one — jumbo. For their morning snacks, ravens pluck small dogs from front yards. If the small dogs should survive the ravens, the coyotes get them. For their safety, you must lock small dogs indoors, 24/7. There they'll become neurotic and bug-eyed, but they'll live. Cats on the other hand, seem to have a knack for surviving these "natural" disasters, but too often wind up as furry little speed bumps on the side of the road, blood oozing from their meowless mouths — victims of passing delivery trucks.

Cats are blind to trucks, just like dogs are blind to me — except I don't go running over dogs. I run by them.

I realized at an early age that I was invisible to dogs. My sister, Beatta, was/is the opposite: not only is she visible to dogs, it seems they can see nothing else. She still carries two small scars where our neighbour's terrier escaped from their house, leaped over me, and seized Beatta by the nose.

There it was, this stupid little dog hanging from her face while she screamed, flapping her arms like she was trying to fly from the scene.

I took one swing at the dog and sent him skittering onto his butt. He scrambled to his feet and looked up at me as if to say, where the hell did you come from? Then he took off like a shot. A raven had landed nearby.

Beatta held her nose while blood streamed from between her fingers, "What did you do that for?" she screamed, and tried to kick me with her boots.

I didn't understand what she meant, but Beatta holds it against me still, like I was somehow responsible for the scars on her nose. Maybe I was. I never told her about how that was the first time I realized I was invisible to dogs.

Then began my invisible encounters with dogs, like fights my friends would get me to break up. With three or four dogs, tearing into each other, someone would yell, "Maryanne, stop them!" and I would dutifully enter the fray but never actually succeed. Sometimes they would stop of their accord, but it gave my friends some kind of kick to see a person so close to danger unharmed by it — sort of like a fire walker not getting burned.

There were also the neighbours with the wolf-dog. It had yellow eyes and a snarl that sounded like it was gurgling blood. It ripped into anyone who passed through their gates. The wolf-dog neighbours thought this fair enough because they posted two big "Beware of Dog" signs as ample warning. If you couldn't read or thought it was a bluff, too bad for you. I, however, regularly climbed their backyard fence to retrieve balls and frisbees. The dog never lifted an eyebrow.

One day, an RCMP Constable came to the wolf-dog neighbour's house. Constable Denis. I watched him unsnap his holster and pull out his gun before he opened the gate. He entered. In order, I heard the blood-gurgling snarl, then four gunshots and three yelps — each shot followed by a yelp, except the last. The shots sounded like firecrackers, but sharper and more contained — little packages of death. I guess that's what bullets are.

Pellets from pellet guns are not quite packages of death — just packages of maiming and pain. I know because I've fired them myself, at my sister's prodding. Beatta has one of those guns and takes delight at firing rounds of pellets into the hides of passing critters — furred or feathered. I'm not a good shot, but I hit a dog once, in the eye.

One day, we were walking to school when two dogs appeared from around some bushes. They were nearly full-grown German Shepherds minding their own business, or minding whatever dogs mind around bushes. However, Beatta threw a rock at them. Why she threw the rock, I can only guess, but they turned, bared their fangs and in about three bounds were on top of her, knocking me over on their way. One had a hold of her leg, and the other her arm. Beatta was screaming.

With my school bag I banged on the arm-chewer's head, then the leg-chewer's. No effect. I tried kicking. They dug in harder. I found the biggest, sharpest stone I could, and with all my might I smashed against the dogs' hind toes, first one dog, then the other. They both let go, yelping. They backed off. One of the dogs had a white eye — blind. I threw the rock and quite by chance, hit its other eye.

The dogs were gone faster than you could cry wolf. I didn't realize my own strength because lying near my sister was a bloodied dog's toe, its large claw distended. Maybe it was pure luck at hitting just right to sever it, especially since a dog's hind foot is smaller than its fore. One of those dogs had limped off with only seven toes holding up its back end. And one of them was blind. Maybe it was the same dog.

Beatta had evil cuts on her legs and some on her arm, but she was okay. She has even less use for dogs now than she did before. I can't imagine why. The really weird thing, of course, is that after her wounds healed, she denied the attack ever happened. She remembers the "nose dog," but not the "leg dog," even though "leg dog" happened after "nose dog," when we were around ten. She doesn't remember how she got the scars on her arm. It was around this time that Carl Danziger started following me home.

Memories don't die in chronological order and I take it nothing is meant to live too long; I'm trying to get through grade twelve. Even though I swear these things are true, my mom says they never happened; that they are a product of my imagination.

Maybe so, but I know what happened the day before yesterday.

I went running after school over the first new snow of the year. Someone had been out earlier on their quad. Dog tracks trailed along beside the quad's. The only person I know who runs their dog while driving their quad is Carl Danziger.

Their tracks went only in one direction so if they hadn't taken "the big loop" around the lake, seventeen kilometres from where I normally enter the trail, I would meet them coming back. It always filled me with dread.

I had run nearly three kilometres, just about to my turnaround point, when I encountered a deer. A dead deer, newly dead, lying in a small clearing; the ravens had not yet found it.

It lay a few feet off the trail. Blood was sprayed across the skiff of snow like red chiffon. I stopped and examined the site more closely. It looked like the quad might have hit the deer. A small hole trickled a frozen comma of blood at the centre of the deer's skull — right between the eyes. Powder burns singed the fur around the hole. A large set of footprints showed that someone had walked around the carcass and stopped at its head. A second set of prints pocked dozens of dancing steps in and around the first. They belonged to a dog.

I turned around and ran back home.

Yesterday, another small layer of snow fell on top of the first. I run till the snow gets too deep. Then I switch to cross-country skis. I don't like it as much as running free-footed along the trail, but I have to do something in winter. Skiing offers almost the same Zen-like experience as running, but skis are cumbersome and distracting — as much in their use, as in their waxing and care. So I relish these last few free-foot runs before the deep snow comes.

There were no fresh tracks, except those of a small fox meandering on and off the trail, and few squirrel runs. As I approached the site of the kill, a dozen ravens squalled and hollered rising skyward but the deer was no longer where it lay the day before. The snow, flecked black with droppings, was scuffed flat. An irregular path pressed into the shallow snow and grasses, snaking into the woods. I followed it, till I came across what was left of the carcass. I then realized it had been yanked there, inch by inch, because of the way the snow was ridged. It would have to have been something big, like maybe a wolf or a pair of coyotes. It was surrounded now not only by raven prints but by canine prints of differing size, shape and quantity as well.

One of the prints had only three toes.

The whining of two-stroke engine drilled its way through the woods. A quad was approaching.

∾∾∾

My boss is Manny Delorme. The first week I worked for him, he gives me this quad. He took it as a payment for something and it's a piece of junk, but if I get it going, it's mine. I can use it too. You don't need a driver's licence for a quad — if you stay off the roads.

I get it going and I'm as happy as a pig in you-know-what. So is Ike.

Ike's my dog. He's a great dog too, a German Shepherd something cross but mostly Shep. He could win shows if they had a German Shepherd something cross category except he's lost a toe on his left hind paw. Or maybe he was born like that. I don't know. He is also blind. He's got two white marbles for eyes. Maybe he can see shapes or light and dark, but not much else. I got him from the dump. I used to go there to shoot things, but not dogs. People leave pets there. They can scrounge food for a while if somebody doesn't pick them up and if the coyotes or ravens don't get them first. I saw a bag of kittens there once. I shot them. They were sick. I took Ike home but Mom wouldn't let me keep him. That's how come I moved out.

The dog needed a name and I always liked the name Ike because I saw this picture of a badge in a book (or TV?) that said "I like Ike." I don't know who Ike was, maybe a politician or something, but I named my dog that right away without even thinking about it. Anyway, Ike loves going for runs with me on the quad. If I time it right, I get to see Maryanne Ravenhurst running too. Maryanne Ravenhurst and those long legs and long hair.

At work, I mostly do brakes and mufflers. Manny does the rest. I was working on a GM half-ton, only a couple of years old. I just replaced the brake pads and Manny says take it for a little spin to make sure they're set right. I'm thinking what if they're not set right, and I wind up in the lake? And then I'm guessing that Manny can do without me, but not the business he would lose if one if his customer's dies if his brakes don't work. So maybe I'm a bit ticked and I peal a bit of rubber around the corner, but I'm barely straightened out again when Constable Denis is flashing his red and blue cherries like night's on fire.

"Hello," I says.

"Whatcha doing Carl?" he says.

"Testing the brakes," I says.

"You stepped on the wrong pedal then Carl. Where's you're registration and drivers licence?" he says.

He knows my licence is suspended, and he knows the truck isn't mine. He knows Manny's going to be really ticked if I don't get back fast. "This is stupid," I say to him.

"Better come with me," he says.

The last thing I need is another run-in with Denis. It wasn't even a month ago but there he was, giving me orders to destroy Ike, or he would be happy to do it himself. So I said, yes, no problem.

But I can't kill Ike. I love him. He needs me. I am his eyes.

I know where there's another dog around who looks just like Ike. So I find him, and I shoot him, and I gouge out his eyes and break off his jaw because it's a different colour. Then I bring him in the RCMP office and park that dog right on Denis' desk hoping the blood will run all over his nice neat stacks of paper.

Of course I have to be more careful about when I let Ike out, and where I go with him. I stick to the woods, the lake trail.

So Denis takes me down the cop shop and charges me with auto theft.

Manny is great about it though. He doesn't fire me and he tells Denis to take it easy, it's partly his fault, Manny's, for telling me to take the truck for a test drive. He tells Denis by the way, to bring his car in, his own car, and he'll give him a real good deal on the winter tune-up special.

So Constable Denis, the tool that he is, brings his heap into the shop. Manny says to me, "It's all yours Kid. Don't screw it up."

This is not a big deal. Anyone can change the oil, rotate the tires and make sure the anti-freeze is good to forty below — that's the special. So I do it, no problem. Okay, one problem — I forget to put the oil cap back on the cam cover accidentally on purpose.

It's just after work and I'm taking Ike for his run. Our usual track is once around the lake, about seventeen kilometres. I look forward to the run as much as Ike. Although he's in it for the exercise, I'm in it for the chance of spotting Maryanne Ravenhurst. Her dad owns Ravenhurst Supplies. I did a B and E there once. Maryanne's supplied, I can tell you that. Perfect. Sometimes I meet her coming; sometimes going; sometimes not at all. She never waves. She never looks at me. Which is just fine by me because I get to stare at her the whole while we're passing and she never knows. It's like I'm invisible to her. How do you get somebody to see you when they won't look? Maybe she's just blind, like Ike. Maybe she knows her way around these trails like he does. Sometimes he's gone for two whole days. Then he returns with a smile on his face and beer on his breath. He's been out partying somewhere. Okay, not beer — blood. He's been out hunting, but hey, that's partying for dogs. He dances around a kill.

Like yesterday I had an accident. I didn't think it was possible, but I was moving at a pretty good clip when I came into a small clearing where a deer got startled and jumped right into the quad. She was a small doe and badly injured. Somehow part of her broke open and sprayed blood all over. I knew that I'd have to kill her, put her out of her misery. I put one bullet right between her eyes.

Ike danced the whole time. Danced in the blood.

I got back in the quad and kept going. Ike came with me for a little while, and then he disappeared. He didn't show up till this morning. My guess is that he went back to the kill. I'm curious to see it now.

There's a bit more snow this evening and I can clearly see that Maryanne has been on the trail ahead of us. My heart beats a little faster. Part of me wants to see her without any clothes on, but mostly I just want her to see me.

So it was quite a surprise when I came into the clearing and there she was, standing near the woods. She looked up and waved for me to stop.

"Carl, come here!" she called.

I just about fell off the quad I turned so hard.

"Look at this," she said.

She was standing over the kill. It was hard to believe that in one day so little would be left of the doe. It was about now that I became aware of a low growling. It was Ike. He was beginning to bare his teeth.

"Shut up, Ike!" I said. He backed off a bit but he kept his forelegs locked stiff, ready.

"Did you kill this deer?" She asked. I suddenly was very visible to her. Naked. She looked me right in the eye.

"No," I lied, looking right back at her. I'm good at lying.

"I think you did. It looks like you ran over it and then shot it."

"I got better things to do than running over deer."

"You and that dog of yours. You just go around killing things."

"What's it to you?"

"You have no respect for things."

"I respect you. I think you're perfect."

"Go! Leave now," she said.

For some reason, her telling me this made me get off the quad. I didn't feel like leaving just yet. It was nice to have this conversation with Maryanne Ravenhurst. "You got real nice legs. From all that running I guess, eh?"

"I'm going to scream."

"How about your feet? You got all your toes?"

"Yes," she said. She was real scared all of a sudden. She was taking little backwards steps. But there wasn't far she could go before backing into a tree.

"Yes, what?"

"Yes, Carl."

"Call me 'Ike'."

"Yes, Ike."

"Take off your shoes."

She stood there.

"I said take off your shoes."

"What are you going to do?" she asked. She was whimpering now. It was kind of pathetic, her hopping on one leg taking a shoe off. First one then the other.

"Now sit."

"Sit?"

"In the snow."

She sat. Ike was showing his teeth. Growling. "Shut up, Ike," I said.

"He can't see me," she said.

"No, he's blind. But he can hear good and smell better."

"I'm invisible to dogs," she said.

"But not to me," I said. "Now your socks."

"My socks?"

"I want to see you feet."

"They'll get cold."

"They'll get cold, what?"

"My feet will get cold, Ike."

"Ike," I said.

And that's when he went for her.

∾∾∾

I thought the judge was pretty kind, considering the unusual viciousness of the crime and the fact that she might have bled to death. Manny did his best for Carl, trying to cover for him. Why he would even bother is anybody's guess. This time I shot the dog, the right dog, with those white orbs staring back at me.

The girl's going to be all right, but no more jogging for her. She was lucky she made it back at all, crawling all that way in the snow, her shoes gone, her toes chewed off. You wonder what the hell happened.

SOLO

There's no explanation for why Megan was terrified of things with eyes, people for instance, who might look at her in public. But she was also afraid of practically everything else: dogs and cats, heights, depths, enclosed spaces, the dark, spiders, snakes, birds and barbed wire. She was cowed by loud noises, too much sun, too much rain, and worried about the poisons in what she ate, drank and breathed. She was terrified by the dust mites that lurked beneath her bed . She was spooked by what hid in her closet, and she had seen strange things crawl out from that crack beside the door to the basement.

"They had long, spikey tails that slithered and slid," Megan insisted.

Her mother would often thunder at her, "Stop exaggerating, Megan Matthews; stop right now!" which would only remind her of the terrors of thunder, as well as its especially awful, bright-striking partner — lightening.

The night she was born, a typhoon tore through her home town of Feton and obliterated the water tower. It landed right between the goat cheese factory and the hospital where she was cradled in her mother's arms. The water from the tower mercifully missed the hospital but it sloshed through the cheese factory rinsing a ton of feta onto the streets of Feton where it stank up the town for weeks. Megan doesn't remember any of this consciously, but what deep scars have gouged their ways into her psyche whenever her mother retells the story?

"How would that affect your psyche?" Megan heard her mother ask plump Mrs. Remple across the kitchen table drinking coffee.

Mrs. Remple didn't reply, just clutched the cup with both her hands and brought it to her lips.

Psyche. Megan didn't know what that meant either, not really, but it sounded scary too. Clearly, the inexplicable events surrounding her birth had inexplicable results. To top it all off, whenever Megan felt particularly upset, the scent of cheese mysteriously arose as real as the night the typhoon tipped the water tower.

Megan was timid. Spooked. Jumpy. Anxious. She thought she would survive only as long as she lived in the safe sanctuary of her home, or better, her room, which was her fortress against those things that wanted to attack her.

Megan shared her fortress with her sister, Allison. Ally often sang to soften the sounds of approaching night and keep the monsters behind the door. She had no fear at all. None. Megan had it all.

Allison was in grade two when Megan went to kindergarten.

Gone was the safety of her home. Of her room. Of her singing sister.

She was thrust into the cold, hostile world of five-year-olds with their nasty little lunch boxes and runny noses. For the first two days, she cowered beneath Miss Haworth's desk and only came out at nap time. On day three, when finally she ventured into the classroom to take a seat at the crayon table, it was Bobby Runnock — she would never forget his name, his red hair and his sneery fishhook of a smile — who dropped a big fat book onto the floor behind her that sounded all the world like a crack of thunder. It sent Megan quavering and sobbing back under the desk, clinging to Miss Haworth's skinny leg. The whole class of snotty-nosed, stinky-cheese brats laughed their fool little heads off. Ha, ha, ha. Very funny. Big joke.

You couldn't pry Megan from under the teacher's desk with a crow bar.

Her mother had to come and get her.

It was good and peaceful and quiet at home — or at least in the safety of her room — as long as she didn't open the closet door. But if she closed her eyes and hummed real loud, whatever lurked, hid, bumped or gurgled anywhere in or near the room would go away. Allison helped with the humming. She'd hold Megan's hand too.

So Megan didn't go back to kindergarten.

But she couldn't avoid grade one.

Grade one came to get her with all the force of the law, society and the dreaded Miss Potts. Miss Potts took it as a personal mission to make all her children feel comfortable in school. She wanted M. J. Collins Junior and Senior Academy to be a harbour away from home, an island of peace and tranquility and knowledge — a nurturing place instead of the hellhole it actually was.

Miss Potts marched across the lawn and dragged Megan from her house kicking and screaming. Her feet barely touched the ground as she hung between the determined teacher and her mother, flapping like laundry on a windy day. Allison followed behind, singing "Silent Night" because she knew Megan liked Christmas, even though it was months away.

As they reached M. J. Collins Junior and Senior Academy, Allison was shrieking "*All is calm*", and Megan was howling like a fire truck when who should she see but Bobby Runnock. It seemed as though he'd been waiting for her. For an entire year.

Still strung between Miss Potts and Mrs. Matthews, Megan stopped howling long enough to be stunned for a moment or two.

Bobby was joined by a chorus of classmates. They chanted together. "Scaredy cat! Scaredy cat! Megan is a scaredy cat!"

Allison stepped out from behind Megan. She walked up to Bobby and said, "Leave my sister alone!" Then bopped him square on the nose.

Blood squirted from him like red ribbons. It was really impressive. Both Miss Potts and Mrs. Matthews dropped Megan and ran to take care of Bobby with his bleeding nose. While they took care of Bobby, Allison took care of the rest of the chorus. She chased them. Those she caught, she also pummeled, screaming "Leave my sister alone!"

She had to be subdued.

When it was all over, Allison was barred from M. J. Collins Junior and Senior Academy and was forced to attend another school, The Sacred Heart of Jesus, a Catholic school where they had special classes for kids with behaviour problems. Allison wasn't even Catholic. They put her on drugs. She didn't sing any more. She was really tired at home and went to bed at seven. She slept like a person in the middle of a very long, dark dream. She barely breathed. It was so sad.

In the meantime, Megan went to M. J. Collins Junior and Senior Academy for two years. She learned to keep her head low, to not look anywhere but down. She learned to wad cotton into her ears to muffle the teasing jeers, and so she wouldn't jump too high at loud noises. She tried not to get too scared. She tried not to wet her pants more than once a week. She wore those skinny little diapers so nobody knew.

But people knew anyway. It was because Bobby Runnock emptied out her backpack onto the school grounds. "What's this?" he said, holding up her spare diaper, the one she kept just in case.

Then it was, "Megan is a Pee Pants; Megan is a Pee Pants."

He put the diaper on his head and wore it like a hat. "Megan is a pee pants." Pretty soon, everybody was saying, "Megan is a pee pants." The place stank of cheese.

Even Mrs. Whithers, her grade three teacher, knew. She also knew that when Megan raised her hand to leave the room it was absolutely essential. She would look at Megan, roll her eyes, let her mouth make that smacking noise and say, "Yes, Megan. You may go."

So it was yet one more time that Megan picked up her backpack where she kept her spare and went into the washroom.

She locked herself inside a stall.

She began to change her diaper. She had one leg in and one leg out.

A strange clattering erupted in the adjacent stall. She froze, standing on one leg like a stork.

A skateboard appeared beneath the stall wall. It bumped into Megan's stork ankle.

A small voice said, "Sorry! I'm so sorry! Just kick it back out. I didn't mean it, honest."

Megan quickly pulled her other leg through the diaper and kicked the board from where it came. She was half-terrified and half-curious. What was a skateboard doing in a toilet stall? Who would take one there?

She lowered her head to peek under the stall, and a pair of deep, dark eyeballs stared straight back at her. She screamed. The person with the eyeballs screamed too.

"I'm sorry! I'm sorry!" the voice said again. "I had to see who else was using a diaper."

"How did you know I was using a diaper," Megan asked the person with the dark eyeballs.

"I could hear it. They make that diaper sound."

It was true. They did. If you knew what to listen for. This person obviously did.

"How come you have to use one?" Megan asked through the toilet stall wall.

"I have a bladder problem," she said.

A skater with a bladder problem. Megan had to see this. She opened the stall door and peeked out.

A dark-skinned, tiny, not-much-taller-than-her-skateboard person stood wearing a great big toothy smile the size of a cantaloupe wedge. Her eyelashes were as long as the bill on her baseball cap — which she wasn't supposed to be wearing.

"They let me wear my hat," she said, "because I don't have any hair on my head." She took it off to show Megan. Sure enough, she was almost as bald as a light bulb. "My name's Veema Surindith. What's yours?" she said, holding out her hand.

"Megan," said Megan. "Megan Matthews."

"I like you Megan," she said. "You and I are going to kick some butt."

Sometimes you meet someone and you know you've met a kindred spirit, that no matter how odd it may look on the outside, on the inside — where it counts — you have a common soul, a belief and hope the world is a good place as long as you have each other to share it with. This would be Veema and Megan.

Veema had been around since the beginning of the school year, and although she was smaller than Megan, she was in grade five, the same as Allison. Veema always wore a rainbow of colours and a hat or cap or toque to match her mood — even a fedora for when she felt mysterious. She rode her skateboard whenever she could and otherwise toted it under an arm. She told her teachers she had a rare bone disease and the board was, like, her wheelchair.

The recess bell rang. They exited the washroom and continued along with Veema on her board, and Megan strolling alongside.

Until Bobby Runnock exited a classroom. "Oh it's Megan Pee Pants!" he said. In an instant, they were surrounded by taunters.

Veema stepped off her board and it popped like magic into her hands. This impressed the crowd. "I am a very, very sick person," she announced. "And I'll show you too." She took off her hat displaying the isolated threads of black hair pressed against her otherwise bald skull. "You want me to BREATHE on you? You'll get what I got!"

"AAAHH!!" The crowd dispersed as though she were the sole carrier of the bubonic plague or something as bad, or even worse.

"Are you really sick?" asked Megan.

"Nah. Except for my bladder of course. I was, that's why I have no hair. It comes in handy if people think I have some weird disease. It's hard getting respect when you're so short."

"I think you're a great height," Megan said.

"Thanks," she said, hopping back onto her board. "Now we can see eye to eye. Coming through!" she yelled. "Breathing real hard! With lots of germs!"

The hallway emptied of stragglers and it smelled just fine

Allison would love Veema, thought Megan. She had to introduce her. So at lunch time, they snuck away from their school yard and stole over to nearby Sacred Heart. They passed the feta cheese factory and the hospital on their way. The rebuilt water tower was squeezed between the buildings.

"You'll really like Allison," said Megan. "I call her 'Ally.' She has to go to this school because she gets mad sometimes."

"Oh, really? I get mad too," Veema said, "So we should be friends."

Sacred Heart of Jesus was separated from the rest of the world by a chain-link fence that reached high as a stop sign. The yard was a riot of students running around or hanging in clumps from the play equipment. Nearby, a twosome of teachers patrolled, keeping a stern eye on things.

But all alone, her back against the school wall, her eyes fixed on the cracked concrete at her feet, leaned Allison.

Megan called.

Allison slouched her way to the fence. The pair of teachers separated. One of them moved slowly and deliberately like a giraffe looking for higher, fresher foliage. She was the type of teacher who, if she went looking for trouble, was sure to find it. Her name was Mrs. Foster. She casually followed in Allison's wake.

Allison looked pale and tired, not like Megan's big sister who sang all the time. Megan tried to cheer her up. "Ally, this is my friend Veema."

"Hi," said Veema, poking her fingers between the links, trying maybe for a two-fingered handshake.

"'Lo," said Allison, staring at Veema's fingers as if they were strange brown worms. Then as though feeling their delicate warmth, Allison reached out and touched them.

Veema smiled.

"We miss you at regular school," said Megan.

"Yes, we'd be in the same class!" said Veema.

"That's nice," said Allison in an empty box sort of way. She constructed a smile upon her face just to let them know she hadn't forgotten what happiness looked like. At least she was trying.

Meanwhile, Mrs. Foster — "Ferocious Foster" as she was not affectionately known — had manoeuvred near, pretending to read a book. You could tell she was pretending because the book was upside down. She bent an ear in Megan's direction and turned a page.

"I told Veema you get mad sometimes," Megan said laughing.

"I do, I really do," said Veema.

"You do?" asked Allison, her eyes growing wide.

"I get so mad, I throw things," said Veema.

"And why are you telling her that?" interjected Mrs. Foster in a decidedly bilious tone.

Megan turned to look up at where the sour voice had come from, and was frozen by the tiny black pupils riding on those long white eyes. "So, so, so . . . " Megan stuttered.

"So Ally doesn't feel so alone," Veema intervened.

"You do not throw things, and never, ever when you're mad — it has nothing to do with feeling alone," said Mrs. Foster. "And who are you anyway?"

"She's my sister's friend," said Allison.

"I don't care if she's the Queen of Sheba," said Mrs. Foster to Allison. Turning to Megan and Veema, she continued. "And you two can take your advice with you and leave — or would you prefer I report you to your principal?"

"I was just . . . " Megan didn't know how to continue.

"Allison, you come with me." Mrs. Foster took her by the arm.

"Come on, we'd better go," whispered Veema. "I think we upset things."

"Leave me alone," yelled Allison, trying to jerk her arm free of Mrs. Foster's twiggy grip.

Two more teachers ran across the school yard towards them.

"You lay one hand on me and I'll, I'll . . . "

"Throw something?" suggested Mrs. Foster.

Although she was about to make a threat, Allison reconsidered. "I won't do anything."

"Allison!" Megan cried.

"I'll be okay," Allison shouted as she was led away.

Veema tugged gently at Megan's arm. "When I get mad at the neighbour's dog, I throw popcorn at her," Veema said. "It works to keep her quiet. I would never hurt her."

"I wish I could throw popcorn at Ally's teachers to keep them quiet," Megan said.

"Ally'll be better soon. You just watch."

But it was Megan's fault that Allison was at Sacred Heart, in that special class, all drugged up, with teachers running to take her away; it was all Megan's fault; she was afraid of everything; she had screamed and cried, and Allison had tried to protect her from Bobby Runnock.

Megan told this to Veema, who said nothing. She just let Megan hold her hand, pretending that she needed Megan to pull her on her skateboard.

They went back to their school. The scent of cheese hung in the air like sweaty old socks.

Snow had begun to fall and Christmas was no longer far away. Allison and Megan had to make their own lunches because their parents were too busy with Christmassy tasks. Mrs. Matthews had begun her Christmas baking and Mr. Matthews was bottling his Christmas wine. Allison's job was to help him wash the bottles — of every size and shape, retrieved from the garage where they had stood like little green soldiers along a shelf. He wouldn't let her help fill them and she would only watch as he laid them in their little coffins in the basement. Then they would reappear one by one on the kitchen table, via the refrigerator, to be emptied a glass at a time by Mr. and Mrs. Matthews. They called it their "Christmas Juice."

Allison was clearly gaining control of her temper, and ever since Megan and Veema's unscheduled school visit, she was improving daily. Even Mrs. Foster had to acknowledge that. She might well be allowed back at her old school early in the new year. That was what she hoped at any rate. She told Megan none of this. It would be a surprise ready for Christmas.

Everyone was getting ready for Christmas, even Mrs. Whithers, Megan's grade three teacher. She decided Megan was a challenge to her perfect world full of snowy fluff and sparkles, where everything had smiley yellow faces and where yuletide decorations were silver, red and green.

She also decided Megan was very shy. That she was sad and lonely.

"You need to pull out of yourself," she said. "You need to sing. And you will sing, for the Christmas concert."

"I can't," Megan said. "I could never sing alone." She was thinking of when she would quietly sing along with Ally, when things were fine, when music filled their room.

"You won't have to sing alone, Deary, not a solo. You will sing a duet — with Bobby Runnock."

The whole class laughed at this announcement, except for Megan. And Bobby Runnock.

Veema and Megan sat together at lunch where Megan told of her treacherous fate — that she was to sing a duet with Bobby. That she would just as soon die as attempt such a feat. That maybe she should run away from home and get a job in a circus, except what would a circus want with a ten-year-old girl who could hardly turn somersaults and was afraid of lions and clowns? Maybe if she could find a good orphanage, she could hide there till she was an old woman of thirty when nobody would care if she sang or not.

"Sometimes you have to be really strong," said Veema. But Megan knew by the look on her face that she was worried too. "Do you mind if I have a drink of your pop?"

"Sure," Megan said, "it's a big bottle. There's lots." Although they weren't allowed to bring glass bottles into school, she had looked for a drink to go with the lunch she had made herself, and having hardly given it a moment's thought, had grabbed a slender green bottle of her parents' Christmas Juice.

"Mmm. Is it ever good," said Veema.

"Yes, it is," agreed Megan. "My dad makes it."

"Tastes sort of like grapes," Veema said, taking another sip.

"'Christmas Juice' he calls it. He never lets us drink it though. It's 'only for grownups' he says."

"And, 'on special occasions' I bet," offered Veema.

"Yeah that, and 'it's too expensive for kids to drink'."

They passed the bottle back and forth taking sips while nibbling on their sandwiches. Pretty soon, they stopped nibbling and just kept passing the bottle.

"I can't sing anything," Megan said. "Except maybe with Ally, when she's singing. Except she doesn't sing anymore."

"Hold it, hold it! Let's think this through. What is singing anyway?"

"It's like talking — only you go high and low."

"There! You can talk — you've got it half beat already," said Veema.

"Except you have to do it to music," Megan said.

"Well then we'll just have to teach you music!" she jumped to her feet. Then quickly sat down. "Whew! I must have got up too fast. I feel a bit dizzy." She stood up again — more slowly and carefully this time.

"Where're you going?" Megan asked.

"To where the music is! Come on!" She pulled Megan to her feet.

Megan was a bit dizzy herself. She was careful to hang on to that bottle. She didn't want to spill any or make a mess. "Where's the music?" She asked, more or less stumbling behind Veema.

"In the music room!" Veema sang, "Where else?"

The music room was in the senior part of M. J. Collins Junior and Senior Academy, and at lunch time was usually filled with guys who needed hair cuts. Or shaves. Or both. They were supposedly in grade eleven or twelve, but looked old enough to be someone's uncle. Megan was usually terrified of them but today for some inexplicable reason she thought going to the music room with Veema was a great idea.

They entered the room. It was filled — and filled them — with cacophonous sounds of two electric guitars, a set of drums, a saxophone, a trombone and a girl screeching into a microphone, banging on a tambourine. The singer, Megan guessed.

In a moment or two, the noise stopped.

A guy with the longest hair and beard, holding a guitar, was the first to speak. "What do you want?" he asked.

"My friend Megan wants to learn to sing," said Veema.

"What?" He acted like he hadn't heard. Maybe he hadn't.

Veema spoke louder. "Sing, you know, la-la-la . . . What she's trying to do." Veema pointed at the girl with the tambourine.

"She wants to learn how to sing," he said to the others. "Do you think we can teach her how to sing?"

"She don't look like a singer, Kahlin," said the girl with the tambourine.

"Well neither do you, Cheryl," Kahlin replied. "Go, aah," he said to Megan.

"Aah," Megan said.

"She can hit a note," said Kahlin.

"Hitting a note is not singing," said Cheryl.

"It's a start," said Kahlin. Then like it was a cue to start a song, they all broke into cacophony again.

"It's the start of a song

It's a song of a start

Yeah, chuga, chuga chug

Yeah

It's the start of a day

It's the day of a start

Yeah, chuga, chuga, chug

Yeah."

They stopped. They stared at Megan. The silence roared.

"Your turn," said Kahlin.

"'My turn, what?"

"To sing," he said.

"She has to sing a Christmas carol," said Veema.

"I can't sing anything," Megan said. She was suddenly growing weepy. If she didn't watch it, tears would soon be falling from her face. They would splash on the floor and make puddles, and the puddles would fill the room and they would all drown.

"You know what she needs?" asked Kahlin.

"What does she need?" asked Veema.

"She needs . . . ," He stopped, raised his hands like he was conducting a symphony, then dropped them.

They all said together, "The Magic Mike!"

"What's the magic mike?" asked Veema.

The drummer tossed a metal rod across the room. Kahlin caught it and handed it to Megan. It was shaped like an ice-cream cone at one end, except instead of ice-cream, it was covered in wire mesh and seemed to be strung together with duct tape. A lone wire hung loose at the other end.

"This is it? It doesn't look very magic to me," said Megan.

"And what does magic look like?" asked Kahlin.

"It's invisible!" Veema shouted just a bit over loud.

"That's what makes it magic!" said Kahlin. "Try it."

"Doh," said Megan.

"Ray," said Kahlin.

"Me," Megan said.

"Fa," said Cheryl.

"So?" Megan asked.

"La," said Kahlin.

"Tee," said Drummer.

"Doh," Megan sang.

And before you could say Magic Mike, Megan was singing. She sang the complete verse and chorus of "O Holy Night" — including the impossibly high note. Her voice soared like an angel. It was beautiful. Allison would have been proud. Her mother would have been proud. Mrs. Whithers would have been proud. Maybe even Bobby Runnock.

Then she threw up. Over everything.

And then Veema threw up. Over everything else.

Kahlin pried the bottle from Megan's fingers, but not the microphone. He opened the bottle. He sniffed. "These kids are drinking wine!" he said. "They're stewed!" He hid the bottle. Cheryl called the nurse. Teachers were informed. Parents were called. The place reeked of cheese.

Megan lay in bed with the spins. Bobby Runnock leered in and out of her fevered focus, singing off-key and horribly. This was worse than a nightmare. It was a daymare. She wanted someone to nail down the room so it would stop trying to dump her out.

Allison came home from school. She carried a maul and a gigantic spike and began driving it into the floor. That's what it sounded like. She was actually just climbing the stairs. However, it had a sobering effect on Megan and her room settled upright and left her only a throbbing pain within her skull — her brain trying to escape its enclosed space. Megan didn't know if this was part of a dream or not. She wished it wasn't. But it was.

What also really happened was after Allison arrived home, she lay a cool cloth on Megan's forehead. She was quiet and confident. "I won't have to go to Sacred Heart for much longer. I'll be coming back to Collins."

"Will you help me practice my song?"

Allison wasn't sure what Megan was talking about but she said, "Of course. It's time I started singing again."

So Allison helped Megan learn the song. They sang together like angels, as long as Megan clutched the microphone. Life was good. Never better.

The only thing that didn't change was Bobby Runnock.

Christmas concert day arrived. Together with Allison and her parents, Megan went to the school gym. Veema was there with her mom, and she was sporting a cool new toque that made her look like a rap star. It was black with silver sequins.

"Are you nervous?" Veema whispered.

"Completely," said Megan.

"Hang on to your mike," said Veema.

"A herd of horses couldn't drag it away." Megan clutched it to her chest.

"See you later and good luck!" She gave Megan a big smile and thumbs up.

Megan went backstage to await her turn. Mrs. Whithers directed traffic and tried to keep the grade twos from peering under the curtain to see where their parents sat.

Suddenly Bobby Runnock was beside her. A small whiff of cheese arose.

"Hi, Pee Pants," he said.

This was unfair. It was not nice either. And even more importantly, it was no longer true. Megan had gone pee-pants-free for almost two months. Why was Bobby doing this to her now? He had almost been civil to her during their rehearsals, and truth be known, he could actually hold a tune. In a reluctant sort of way, she was glad he was singing with her. Despite her Magic Mike, she wouldn't want to go it alone.

"That is not my name," said Megan.

"I know it isn't. I'm just trying to bug you. Are you still carrying that thing around?" he said referring to the microphone.

"So what if I am."

"It looks ridiculous. I looks like you're trying to be some kind of rock star or something."

"I'm not, I just happen to like it."

"It's not even plugged in. Can I see it?"

"No."

"I just want to hold it for a sec."

"I said no, now leave me alone."

"Aw come on, what am I going to do, eat it?"

"Oh, all right." Megan handed Bobby the microphone.

"Jeez, this thing weighs a ton. You could use it like a bar bell," he said pumping it up and down as though he was working on his pecs.

"Okay, you can give it back now," said Megan.

"What's all this tape holding it together for?" He began to unravel it.

"Don't!" Megan tried to grab it back.

Bobby was enjoying his taunt. "You want it? Come and get it!" He held the microphone high over his head.

"Bobby! Give it back!"

"See if you can get it from there," said Bobby, throwing the microphone onto a ledge high above a backstage curtain. There it teetered.

"Bobby!"

"What? Can't you sing without it?"

"As a matter of fact, no!" exclaimed Megan.

"Aw-w, poor Pee Pants, she can't sing without her mikey."

"Hush you two!" Mrs. Whithers said to them. She appeared from nowhere and clutched a pair of grade-two angels by the backs of their broken wings. "You're on next!" she said as one of the angels broke free from her grasp and began climbing the backstage curtain.

The sudden tension on the curtain caused a certain unsteadiness on the ledge above it. Megan watched as the Magic Mike tumbled end over end in slow motion from where it had lain. She watched in further horror as she saw where it was going to land. And indeed it landed exactly on the spot occupied by Bobby Runnock's head, hitting him square there and exploding in a hundred different directions.

A moment later, as Bobby lay unconscious and the microphone lay in a zillion pieces, the curtain opened to reveal Megan standing alone on the centre of the stage. From somewhere in the darkened gym, an out-of-tune piano jangled the opening notes to "O Holy Night". Megan stood frozen. The piano stopped. Began again. Still nothing. The audience stirred uneasily.

Suddenly a voice that only Megan could hear, a voice that belonged to her friend Veema said, "You can do it." At least

Megan thought that she was the only one who could hear it, because true friends work that way — they can talk to you and you can hear it when no one else can. But for sure what really did happen was a toque suddenly landed on the stage in front of her. It was black and studded with silver sequins.

Megan immediately recognized the toque and knew that her friend was sitting in the audience with her bald head showing for all to see, and that if Veema had the courage to live with a bald head and diapers, then she, Megan, could sing a Christmas carol. Solo.

So she sang. All three verses. And hit the high notes.

Megan did not go on to become the leader in her own band, like people do in their fantasies. But she sang alto in a choir and learned to be herself, and to smell cheese only when it was placed on a plate in front of her. She learned not to be afraid of many things, including Bobby Runnock, who did in fact become a musician, but one who did not stink as a human being quite so much.

Allison grew up to become the kind of teacher she never had, and although she remained as passionate as ever, she was thoughtful and kind as well.

And Veema . . . well Veema remained Megan's constant friend and came to be the special protector to others who needed her unique and wondrous way of being on the planet throughout her short, but powerful life. Megan would never forget her.

BIG BALLOON

It may be that one Christmas is much like another — a diorama inside a glycerin-filled jar where snowflakes fall as memories — that giddy feeling sleep will never come, the thrilling mounds of red and green wrappings beneath the sparkling tree, the pungent smell of cat-pee spruce mixed with roast turkey and peppermint, aunts with red-cheeked smiles and uncles with whiskey breaths, cousins racing in and out of forbidden rooms — all ending somewhere on the rink, or the snowy hill under the brilliant night sky filled with diamonds.

But when Thomas was young — very young, maybe four — one Christmas stands out from among the rest: The Year of the Big Balloon. Although it was wrapped, he knew it was a balloon and he knew it was for him — his older sister had already outgrown the training wheels on her bicycle and had long since lost interest in such things as balloons.

"Balloons are for babies," she said.

"I'm not a baby, I'm a little kid," said Thomas, always careful about small distinctions.

In his memory the balloon was absolutely gigantic but in fact was no larger than a basketball. Yet it didn't fit beneath the tree; it hung in the air like magic. Wrapped in tissue, tethered by a length of string to the floor, it gently swayed back and forth when someone walked by or opened a door. He didn't know what it was made of — and because his memories are often in black and white, doesn't even recall the colour — but it was partially filled with helium and would hover slightly above his head without rising higher or falling lower.

It was also very durable and put up with a lot of his abuse. He rode it like a horse. He kicked it like a football. And he attacked it like a punching bag. Finally, at night, he let it hover above his bed like a guardian angel. All in all it was fabulous — almost human, for he taught it to come to his bidding from all the way across a room.

"Come!" he would say and hold one hand, then the other rubbing them together.

And truly, some mysterious force — or ion polarization — would gradually carry the balloon in his direction. This was better than having a pet. You didn't have to feed it or clean up its poo. It never barked or meowed or made messes in the bottom of its cage. It was silent, and floated near you, always.

However, you did have to be careful around sharp objects — something, unfortunately, that Thomas was not. And by mid-January, the balloon had shrunk somewhere between soccer ball and softball size, and now hovered knee-high — the perfect height for small boys to slay things with their mother's scissors. It was an accident, of course, that happened on his way to the kitchen table to cut out pictures from a catalogue. Thomas destroyed the balloon nevertheless, as children always do to their favourite things.

Time wears a moth-eaten cloak full of memory holes.

Late in the spring that followed the Christmas of The Big Balloon, Thomas stood in his aunt's living room wearing his Sunday clothes although it was not Sunday. Others also stood in his aunt's living room or sat in her over-stuffed couch and easy chair. Sombre and solemn, they smelled of mothballs and shoe polish. They too were dressed in their church-going clothes.

A fireplace leaned against the wall in the living room, not a real fireplace but the sort with a light bulb and some motorized twisting mechanism that hummed and caused a flickering behind orange tempered isinglass. It was turned on for special occasions and clearly this day was special, for the fake fire hummed and flickered, and this made Thomas happy.

Above the humming fire was a mantle place — a shelf, made by Thomas' uncle — and on the shelf was a picture containing four smiling faces, boys ranging in ages of about seven to twelve. Thomas' cousins.

"There's Elliot . . . and Lewis . . . and Aidan . . . and . . . who's that one?" said Thomas pointing at the picture.

"Tommy, you know who that is," said his mother, "that's Jamie."

Thomas' aunt ran sobbing from the room. Thomas wondered why his aunt was suddenly in such a hurry. Maybe she knew who Jamie was, after all he was standing with his other cousins in the picture.

"Who's Jamie?" said Thomas.

Thomas' Uncle gave Thomas a searing scowl before following to comfort his wife.

"Jamie gave you the big balloon for Christmas. You must remember Jamie," said Thomas' mother.

But Thomas doesn't remember Jamie. There is an empty space in Thomas where the memory of Jamie should be. He remembers the big balloon and how it hovered and bounced, but nothing of Jamie. This was Jamie's funeral, his wake. He'd died earlier in the week, having been hit by a speeding car on the gravelled street. He was on his way to Thomas' house to babysit — something he'd frequently done. Thomas had followed Jamie around like a puppy. And Jamie had doted on Thomas.

Or so I'm told.

I don't actually remember any of this. I don't remember Jamie doting on me. I don't know why I can't remember him, but I can't. Nothing.

High school in no way prepares you for university, and university in no way prepares you for life. For one thing, a stunning array of people grows larger, more peculiar and sometimes, more beautiful. Shivaun, for instance, with long blonde hair and eyes the colour of a warm sea — the Caribbean say, or the Gulf of Mexico. They are as deep and unfathomable too, and if you aren't careful, you'll fall in.

I wasn't careful.

This was okay because she threw me a rope — made of poetry. It was a tough read but somebody (other than Keith Watson that sleek, arrogant slimeball) had to do it.

Keith is from the right side of the tracks. It is called Valley Meadows, a semi-rural community devoted to spawning the horsy set, their dogs and fleets of BMWs. The smallest mansion in the area covers half an acre — not including the barns, kennels and four-car garages.

I, on the other hand, come from a place called, the Lower Flats (the Pits by some) which is the muddy bottom of the aforementioned Valley Meadows, filled with railway tracks, warehouses, bars, pool halls and greasy spoons all surrounded by clapboard bungalows that hunker low on twenty-five-foot lots.

Shivaun though is a farm girl. You'd never guess it by looking at her but she could not only drive the grain truck, she could dismantle it with a pair of vise grips and a screwdriver. How she came to appreciate poetry is beyond me. But then many things are free of my comprehension, this being a small example of one.

We have been dating for a couple of months and Shivaun suggests we go to a poetry reading.

"A poetry reading!" I sneer. I'm still a Lower Flats/the Pits kind of guy. I have my dignity. I don't do poetry readings.

But, of course, I'm in love with Shivaun, her long blonde hair and her impenetrable deep sea-blue eyes.

"Jump!" she says.

"How high?" I beg.

"It starts at 7:00," she says.

"I'll see you there," I say. Shamelessly.

But my car won't start. The car is a relic from the days of the Dukes of Hazard, a 1977 blue Camaro — a gift from my uncle Jake — and a story for some other time.

I have to walk. Two kilometres.

When I arrive — late — at the theatre, I see a black BMW in the parking lot. I know it belongs to Keith Watson. Keith Watson is the kind of guy who goes to poetry readings — just to meet the kind of girl who goes to them.

Girls like Shivaun.

When Keith Watson says one thing, he usually means another — depending on the gender of the person to whom he says it. If he says, "How are you?" to a guy, he really means, "Drop dead you low-life scum." If he says, "How are you?" to a gal, he really means, "Want to go to bed?" or words to that effect. He has a face like a typewriter, an ancient instrument with a fixed bulky smile. It has small metal hammers embossed with letters from the alphabet that slap through an inky tape to place printed text upon a page. This would be how Keith Watson works words.

The poetry reading is in a small theatre called The Blackhole. It is really just a large room, no larger say, than one of the living rooms in Valley Meadows. It is, however, appropriately named because of its distinctive décor: the floor is black, the walls are black, and the ceiling is black. It is a black hole. There is only one light on in this room. And it shines on The Poet.

I know that somewhere within these black walls (and ceiling and floor) sits Shivaun. And Keith Watson. My gripping fear is that she sits with him holding his hand in empathetic embrace with The Poet's urgent self-exposition.

The Poet. Of course you can see nothing but The Poet. He consumes all the radiant energy in the room. Surely there will be a break in his interminable droning, when the lights will be turned on and I will find her — them.

"Never trust a man with a typewriter between his teeth!" quoth The Poet. "He will devour you whole and spit out your bones." He is speaking of himself of course, and how The Poet feeds upon his feeders. He is nevertheless driving an icy spear through my figurative heart. I picture Keith Watson and his dictionary smile, each of his teeth tattooed with a letter of the alphabet.

He is biting Shivaun on the ear.

"I began my career as a chemist," says The Poet. "But I discovered that chemicals are very stupid. You put two chemicals together and they always do the same thing. You put two words together, and you never know what they're going to do."

Exactly, I am thinking. Then the lights come on.

Typewriter Mouth speaks — to Shivaun. She answers. You never know what words will do. They tangle in syntax, tear and eviscerate. They are being subsumed by the black walls (and ceiling and floor) of The Blackhole. I am being tortured by chemistry — or — being run over by a grain truck — by both its back wheels. Followed by a BMW. I am a speed bump.

I get up to leave. Shivaun sees me. She smiles as though she is surprised.

Yes, of course you are surprised, I tell myself. Surprised that I showed up and caught you in the verbiage of Keith Watson.

She begins to cross the floor — the black floor of The Blackhole — heading towards me.

"Tom!" she calls. "Tommy!"

I cannot scuttle fast enough to the door. But I am gnarled in a jam of warm smudgy bodies. A clutch of young women encircle The Poet, The brilliant Poet who looks out beyond them hoping perhaps for something beyond his reach. Like the door. The Poet and I are trapped.

Shivaun kicks me in the back of the leg.

"Ow!"

"Where were you? I had to sit with Keith Watson all night!"

"You didn't have to," I say.

"I was waiting for you, but you didn't show up. I don't like being stood up." There is a decided edge to her voice, like the side of glacier that has just broken free.

"My bus was late," I say. "I didn't stand you up."

"Well, where are you going now?"

"I don't know. You seem to be with him." I nod towards Keith Watson who is rapidly closing.

"You guys want a ride?" he asks.

"Yes, please," says The Poet suddenly including himself in our would-be ménage à trois.

Moments later, The Poet and I are crammed like soft luggage in the back of Keith Watson's car. Keith and Shivaun are pilot and co-pilot, clamped in the front bucket seats.

"Are there any bars in this town?" The Poet wants to know.

"I think everybody wants to go home," answers Keith Watson. Then, half-turning, and out the side of his mouth, he asks me, "Where can I let you off?"

"The nearest bridge," I say, thinking that if I don't jump from it, I can at least burn it after I cross.

"You can drop me off there too," says Shivaun.

"Is there a bar on the bridge?" asks The Poet.

"Wouldn't you like a ride home?" Keith Watson asks Shivaun.

"No, we have to finish our fight," she says glancing at me.

These words send leaping blood through my heart — its dorsal aorta — in effervescent hope — you put two words

together and you never know what they're going to do —
because later in the evening, watching the ice-filled stars from
the bedroom window, we did other things but we didn't finish
the fight. We don't finish the fight. We will never finish the fight.
It will be what binds us together forever and always, no matter
what.

Even if she gets pregnant.

Which she does.

Shivaun sits, half-prone, her belly pointing to heaven. The
pregnant Shivaun is even more beautiful than the pre-pregnant
version — in an earth goddess sort of way: her hair shines, her
nose brightens, her hips and face fill, her breasts enlarge, as does
her gait, and her voice deepens. It is the voice of calm but
absolute authority. It not only transcends gender, it transcends
species. She could command a herd of anxious cats through a
dog pound. For a boy from the Lower Flats, hers is the most
reassuring voice in the world.

I am not, however, prepared for the shower.

Shivaun's regular/normal method of bathing is precisely
that — bathing — reclining in a tub filled with hot sudsy water,
her belly rising above the bubbles like a tropical island ringed
in surf. It is a peaceful, relaxing and eminently fertile sight. Site.
I, on the other hand, am not happy unless the water passes over
me once and only once in the shower like a stream passes over
a stone.

"I've never understood the logic of a bath," I tell her.

"I like getting hot all over at the same time — not scalding
my head while freezing my feet — and then just lying there.
It's very relaxing."

"Yes, but your water's dirty."

"Yours is dirty by the time it gets to your feet too. Anyway,
I don't pee in it, Tom. I soak in it. And I rinse when I'm done."

"So do I."

"But that's all you do. You climb into the shower, squirt yourself, then climb out of the shower."

Nevertheless, as the time draws near, the sides of the bathtub become Everests of resistance and grow increasingly difficult for Shivaun to scale once she is recumbent. So she has decided to shower.

The water roars from the shower head like a wet bus on a busy street — I never knew they made so much noise. But it is working hard — doing its job — scalding her head and freezing her feet. It occurs to me that there are parts of Shivaun's body that she can no longer reach, and that perhaps I should offer to help.

As I open the bathroom door, however, Shivaun is stepping from the shower. The shower curtain hides all but one leg and a belly blushed by heat and hovering like a Great Big Balloon. The cool air rushes in with me.

"Close the door!" she cries.

I close the door and along with the billowing steam, I find what I had forgotten: The Big Balloon was red.

Then the rest of her emerges from behind the curtain.

"What's the matter?" she says. "You look like you've seen a ghost."

I get all soggy hugging my wet wife.

"We're going to name him Jamie," I whisper into her ear.

"What if it's a girl?" she says stepping back.

"Then we'll name her Jamie Shivaun."

It is settled like that — agreed upon and approved. No discussion ensues. The unborn child, whatever its gender, will bear the name Jamie in honour of the dead cousin I cannot remember.

The day arrives. Barely. It is 5:30 AM on a foggy April morning. The contractions are twenty minutes apart and Shivaun is staring a strange, other-worldly blank stare at a blank wall. I have just returned from the bathroom for the tenth time that night. It is as though I am pregnant too. She looks at me, summons an alien basso profundo voice and says, "Get the car."

"Getting the car" actually means the process of removing it from its storage place, a neighbour's garage — I wouldn't think of leaving it on the street — and bringing it around to the front door where a small suitcase waits for the inevitable event.

I get the car. We load up and leave.

From Lower Flats, we navigate through the early morning fog of Valley Meadow. Shivaun is panting through her contractions like a puppy dog — performing her Lamaze breathing techniques — when a strange thing happens: the car dies.

Now, aside from the time it wouldn't start before the poetry reading — and I don't want to dwell on the psychic implications here — the blue Camaro has never been anything but reliable to both me and my uncle Jake. True, it is a pig. It belches and farts noxious fumes into the atmosphere depleting the ozone layer with the best — or worst — of them. Perhaps Mother Earth was muttering her say. But it could go like a hot damn. Until now. The dash lights up like a Christmas tree. I turn the key. Nothing.

We roll to a halt. The silence is broken only by Shivaun's panting. Then she stops, and the only sound is my heart slamming against my ribcage.

"Why did you stop?"

"I didn't stop — the car did."

"I can see that," she says. "If I don't get to the hospital in twenty minutes, I'm going to have the baby on the middle of the highway."

She would too.

I spring out of the car and turn to face the oncoming traffic. There is none — nothing in either direction. I think briefly of pushing the car to the hospital but know that I could never get her there in twenty minutes. I scan the horizon. A vague beam of lights twitches in the distance. I don't care to whom or what those lights belong, I will stop that vehicle or it will turn me into a speed bump. I don't care if it is a Mack truck or a Volkswagon, it is going to taxi us to the hospital while there still is only two of us to taxi.

It draws nearer. It is not a Mack truck. It is something smaller. I wonder if it will try to rip around me. I make myself as big as I can, jumping up and down waving my arms as though I was leading calisthenics for the football team.

The vehicle slows. It's a sports car — a BMW — a Beamer like Keith Watson's. It is now close enough to see the driver. He smiles crookedly. His face is punctuated with a question mark.

It is Keith Watson.

Keith Watson is not alone in his car. He shares it with another person and two large golf bags. I explain the situation. He pulls out his cell phone.

"Can I call you some help? We're on our way to Eagle Point. We've booked a cabin there and thirty-six holes. We're in kind of a hurry."

I eye the back seat.

"The trunk's loaded with coolers," he adds, implying the clubs can't be moved.

By now, Shivaun has arrived at the car. She opens the passenger door.

"Get out," she commands. Her voice rattles the golf clubs. Keith Watson's passenger takes one look at her great Big Balloon and scrambles from the car.

"We won't be long," I say to the stranger as Shivaun takes his place and I extract one of the golf bags from the back seat and dump it on the road. "Do you know where the hospital is?" I ask Keith.

"Of course, my dad is chief surgeon . . . "

"We have about ten minutes, fifteen if we're lucky. Try not to kill us on the way," I say.

"Oh God!" says Keith Watson, putting his car in gear. "Oh God!"

Shivaun begins another round of panting.

"So, how you been?" I ask Keith Watson as nonchalantly as I can.

"Tell her not to have the baby here, okay?"

"You okay, sweetie?" I ask Shivaun.

She nods.

"She promises not to have the baby here if you promise not to hit any bumps too hard."

"Oh God!" says Keith Watson.

"Oh God!" echoes Shivaun.

"What's the matter?" I ask.

"My water broke."

"What's that?" asks Keith.

"Her water broke," I say.

"Yes, but what does that mean?"

"It means I'm wet," Shivaun growls.

"It means the sac that carries the fetus in embryonic fluids for nine months has now ruptured. It means that birth is imminent. It helps lubricate the vaginal canal. It's kind of messy though. It means your car is going to need some serious detailing on the passenger seat." I am amazed at how calm and articulate I am. Given the circumstances. "So, you go to many poetry readings these days?" I ask.

"Poetry readings are for guys like you," says Keith Watson.

"And Jamie," says Shivaun.

"Who's Jamie?" he asks.

"If it hadn't been for the poetry reading, Jamie might never have happened," says Shivaun rubbing her hands over her belly.

"'You put two people together, and you never know what they're going to do,'" I say, paraphrasing The Poet.

"Oh, oh, oh, OH!" Shivaun suddenly wails frantically trying to perform her Lamaze breathing at the same time.

"Hang on! Hang on!" Keith pleads. "We're just about there."

I can't remember if I thank Keith Watson before he vanishes amid a squeal of tires, or if I even manage to wave. I am too busy ushering Shivaun through Admitting then onto the delivery room. Before I enter, I don the mask and gown thrust on me by the duty nurse.

But I am there in time to see the tiny purple face squeeze from the impossible space between Shivaun's legs then expel the rest of his perfect body from her womb. I watch as Jamie inhales his first breath upon the planet — he'd been holding it for nine months — then holler his hello. The nurse places him upon Shivaun's chest. Mother and child are doing fine.

A few hours later, after Shivaun's family has oohed and awed, presented their gifts and gone through all the motions that grandparents, uncles and aunts go through before they run out of ways of making fools of themselves and leave, my mother and sister appear. They too bear gifts. My sister has her guitar and plays a birthday song. It is just like my sister to somehow steal focus, but my mother brings Shivaun a "Snuggli," a baby-carrying device which is the third of its kind she's received.

"Have you decided on a name yet?" she asks.

"Jamie," I say.

"Oh, Jamie! That's a wonderful name, isn't it Jana?"

"Beautiful," says my sister.

"You had a cousin named Jamie," says my mother, "remember him?"

"No, not really," I say. "I just remember the balloon."

"What balloon?" she says.

"What balloon?" asks my sister.

"Yes, what balloon, Tom?" asks Shivaun.

I tell the story of the Year of the Big Balloon. This time I tell it in first person. Through it all, Jamie sleeps.

THE GOLDEN HEART

Glennis is Gregory's mom. She's a social worker for an NGO that houses battered women, a job where fashion consciousness is not a high priority. It's not even a low priority. Glennis wears long-sleeved sweaters — always — usually turtlenecks, often with a black vest with floral patterns and denim slacks all co-ordinated in earth tones. But late in the summer, she takes Gregory shopping.

"We'll get you some cool clothes for school," she says.

Gregory knows she's not talking about temperature. He doesn't know how to tell her that cool doesn't even mean cool anymore — at least not the way she thinks it does. But he goes along anyway. He loves his mom. She tries.

He doesn't really care what she gets him because he's got his blue and white football jacket. When it comes to fashion the jacket's all that really counts as far as Gregory is concerned. Next year, if all goes well, he'll get the leather version. At most, only twelve of them are handed out at a time, and in a school population of fourteen hundred, it singles you out — says you're special: you've made the team.

In grade nine, he tried out for senior football and because of his size and speed, he actually made third-string defensive back and kick-off special team. Most rookies are in grade ten.

When you're a rookie, you do all the grunt work: you haul the water and practice gear out to the field and back; you make sure the towels are in the laundry bin after showers; you clean up the team bus; you do all that plus anything else the seniors ask — and you do it all with a smile. Then, after your rookie season, you get the team jacket. You've earned it.

Gregory puts his jacket on in the morning. He doesn't take it off at supper. He wears it doing his homework.

"Greg, it's a very nice jacket but you're not wearing it to bed," his mother says.

"I know," says Gregory.

On Saturdays Gregory hangs out with his buddies — Josh, Earl and Brandon. He's known them since kindergarten. Gregory is the only one with the blue and white team jacket.

Girls have not yet interfered with the dynamics of the foursome. They pretend they are the renegade crew of the Starship Realize and as they enter Ezone Arcade to play TerrorMatrix, their preferred game, they say things like, "Radiation levels are within acceptable limits." Much of their language is coded like this. "Radiation levels" for instance, refers to the opposite sex.

They think this is very funny.

This coded humour is the glue that binds the group together. One of Gregory's secret dreams is to become a comedian. A comedian like Evan Rude who is the star of a sketch comedy show called Skitz. Gregory loves to make people laugh. Thus far, however, his success at this is limited to Josh, Earl and Brandon.

Drinking from large plastic cups filled with sugar-laden, artificially-flavoured, multi-coloured slushed ice called — remarkably enough — slushies, they sit at a mall food court table and recount last night's Skitz.

In one sketch, Evan Rude plays a Martian who stops off at earth for a cup of coffee. He tries to pay for his coffee with Martian currency, a dorik. But the earth waitress — a bosomy blonde — thinks he is being fresh in making a vulgar play on words. And she wants him to pay in dollars.

"But I'm a Martian," says Evan. "I don't know how many doriks are in a dollar."

"Then I'm going to have to ask you to leave Mr. Marshall . . . "

"Martian, Martian," corrects Evan.

" . . . Mr. Marshall, vacate the premises now, and take your dorks with you," she says.

Gregory and his buddies remember the skit word for word.

"Venting plasma," says Josh.

"Yes," says Gregory. "Primary."

In their code they agree that Evan Rude is indeed a very funny man.

After supper Gregory helps Glennis with dishes. He always washes. His mom prefers to dry. "Have you got change for a dorik?" Gregory asks.

"What?"

"There's thirteen doriks in a frigate," says Gregory.

"A frigate's a boat," says Glennis.

"No, it's like a Martian dollar."

"What are you talking about, Greg?"

"You know — what you spend — money. A dorik."

"There's no need for offensive language."

"Dor-ik! Dor-ik! Not dork! It's not supposed to be offensive — it's supposed to be funny."

"Well it's not funny in the least." With that Glennis slams a cupboard door.

"It was funny last night when Evan Rude said it."

"I don't know how you can watch that stuff."

"It's easy. Josh and Early and Brand watch it too."

"You don't have to like everything your friends like," she says.

"Yes I do — that's why we're friends," say Gregory.

Glennis knows there's no point in pursuing this. "I'm going out for a smoke," she says.

Along with her long-sleeved sweaters, she wears her old-fashioned name — Glennis. It means fair and holy. Glennis feels neither. She doesn't know why her parents named her that. There is no one named Glennis in the family — or none that she's aware of. It makes no sense to her.

There is not a great deal of her life that does make sense — not her name, not her job, not the poor unfortunate people she sees as clients, who are even poorer and more unfortunate than she. Not even her son, Gregory, makes sense — neither literally with his silly jokes, nor physically insofar as he exists at all. He was the result of a single-night passionate encounter when she was nineteen with a man whose face she cannot recall. She tries to see something of that man in Gregory but fails. Despite being over six feet tall, Gregory has decidedly feminine features — hers. She is grateful that despite his abysmal attempts at humour, he is a good boy with a sweet disposition. He helps with the dishes without being asked. She knows more than full-well that he could just as easily be cranked out on crystal meth like half the children of her single-parent clients. She knows this but still worries; "That," she tells herself, "is what mothers do."

But by far her biggest worry is not about Gregory at all: it's about herself.

She doesn't know how things got to be the way they are. Evan Rude and dorks. When Gregory was younger, evenings revolved around baths and story time. Glennis smiles at the thought of Gregory bouncing into bed, insisting on his favourite story — "The Golden Heart". Then she frowns recalling its gruesome content. Perhaps "The Golden Heart" was at the root of all her problems. She wonders where the book itself is. She hasn't seen it for years. She speculates how and when it disappeared. In a fluttering moment, she is unsure if it existed at all — like the men she would bring home from time to time, ostensibly for Gregory's approval, all of who eventually vanished beneath his indifferent gaze. She concludes he was probably doing her a favour. She hasn't had a date in years.

But the story, why would a four year-old like such a story? In the first place, it seemed to be more of a "girls'" story — what with the princesses and all — a fairy tale really. It even began "once upon a time."

In it, the princess fell hopelessly in love with the prince who soon became king when his father died, and he made her his queen.

While the king loved his new queen, he also loved his sister — the princess, the queen mother and each of his subjects too. He inspired loyalty and faith through his love and was said to have a golden heart to accommodate them all.

Meanwhile, although his love for the queen continued unabated, she pondered how it was the king could love her and his sister and his mother and each of his subjects to inspire such loyalty and faith. She wondered if he indeed had a heart of gold till finally one night while the king slept, she poured a sleeping potion into his ear so that he would not awaken no matter what the disturbance.

Then she took a knife and cut open the king's chest to see for herself the king's golden heart. But although it beat strongly, she could see it was a heart that looked like any other. So she cut open the heart itself, and sure enough, there inside, she found it was lined with gold.

The young queen was very happy for she now understood that the king was capable of all his love — including and especially his love for her.

But as she began mending the gaping wounds and closing up his chest, the king's heartbeat grew weaker and weaker. The king would surely die.

Of course, this being a fairy tale, the ending is a happy one because the young queen rallies the kingdom for a great big love-in to resurrect the king and they all live happily ever after.

It bothered Glennis then that her son should take such delight in what seemed to her a particularly lurid tale, despite its overly optimistic and unlikely ending, just as it bothers her now that he might uncover the lurid reality of her own life.

She butts her cigarette in the can she keeps by the door for that purpose. She tells herself she's trying to quit but the time never seems to be right.

"I'm sorry I yelled at you," she says returning to the kitchen.

"When did you yell?"

"About the doriks."

"Oh, that. You just didn't get it. I guess you had to be there."

"Yes. I guess you did," says Glennis. She is immediately struck by how he has already forgiven — or at least forgotten — her transgression. He is a loving son. "Do you remember a story I used to read you, The Golden Heart?"

"The what?"

"Oh, never mind," she says. He's forgotten.

At football practice, Gregory misses most of his coverages and coach Ronstad makes him run ten minutes of bleachers — and it is hot today. Brutal. But it has built in him an enormous appetite. They eat spaghetti for supper which he shovels down, and afterward helps with the dishes. His mom is in a weird mood, first yelling at him, then apologizing.

He collapses onto his bed. He is just going to rest before he does his homework. His mind drifts. Of course he remembers The Golden Heart. It had just taken him a moment to recall, and by then, his mom had dismissed the topic. What a stupid story, he thinks. Next week they have to dissect a frog at school. It is a giant frog, deep black inside; he falls. Falls. Falls.

Gregory awakes confused — in the dark. He checks the clock. It is 12:08 AM.

He has to go to the bathroom.

A blue light flickers and voices emanate from the living room so he assumes Glennis is watching something on TV, or has fallen asleep in front of it as she often does.

The bathroom door is slightly ajar. A thin white light wedges unevenly through the crack to lean against the hallway wall. It is not the usual bathroom light but something smaller — unsteady. Gregory hears some vague stirring within. Then a sigh. Or perhaps a sob. He's not sure. He would normally have called to announce he is in a hurry — instead he freezes.

The sink is partially visible. On it a candle flickers. He edges closer and peers through the crack. He watches as his mother holds a pin in the flame till it's a vivid orange. Then she takes the glowing point and presses it into her left arm — not the veined side — but above the back of the wrist. He can see a small black globe of blood rise from her flesh.

She is so engrossed in her actions, she still does not see him. Her eyes are wide with pain and wonder. She sets the needle aside and dabs at the blood with a piece of gauze, then takes it up again to hold it into the flame.

Gregory can see three or four fresh wounds with small black beads rising from them. The texture of his mother's arms are like the shadows on the moon's surface. For an absurd moment he remembers being wrapped in those arms and being laid into bed.

Gregory flicks on the bathroom light switch. Glennis jumps. Under the harsh light, the black beads become a brilliant red.

"What are you doing, Mom, looking for gold?" says Gregory. He slams the bathroom door closed.

He still needs to go to the bathroom so he goes out the back door and in the cold dark night, pees on the lawn.

Moments later, while Gregory is still mid-stream, Glennis stumbles out wearing her housecoat.

"I'm sorry, Gregory. I'm sorry," she says. "It's not what you think."

"How do you know what I think," Gregory says, zipping up his fly. Then he pushes past her returning inside the house.

The next morning at breakfast Gregory wears his blue and white team jacket. He has cut each of the sleeves into long lengths of ribbon that hang down from the shoulder.

"Good morning," he says as though nothing has happened.

"What did you do to your jacket?" says Glennis.

"I think it looks funny," Gregory says, "like your arms." With that, Gregory picks up his books and goes off to school.

At practice he is vicious in his coverage and misses nothing. In two weeks he's first-string. He cuts his jacket sleeves totally off. So do the rest of the juniors. It's a macho thing. They're hauled before the principal — asked why.

"Go ask my mom," says Gregory.

He has a fist fight with Josh.

On Saturdays he no longer hangs with his kindergarten buddies.

He has a secret to hide, and it's easier to hide things alone.

Blood and Camping

R ed is not an accidental colour. It is the colour of blood. It pumps through our veins and flows from our bodies. When it stops flowing from men, they are either healing or dead. It's the colour of war. You can laugh at the passing of time and the events that occur in it, but you can never laugh at red. Red is on purpose. Primary. The colour of Mars and of my dad.

I remember owning a pair of patent leather red shoes when I was four or five. Dad must have bought them for me — my mother never would have: too showy. I often wondered how the two of them came to be together. Opposites attracting I guess. They had nothing in common. They obviously converged on the bed though, producing me and my brother a year apart — me first, then him.

Dad owned a lot of red, from cars to fishing lures. Mom was always slightly embarrassed by the cars. Dad's official excuse was that people can see them better — a safety issue. He also thought fish could see his lures better. Maybe they could — never mind they are colour blind. Fish are carnivores and there is something carnivorous about the hue inside flesh. At any rate, when I think of Dad, I think of red. I think of red and I think of fishing. He loved both.

He'd just suffered his first heart attack. He was forty-one.

I had just caught the first smear of red on tissue paper between my legs in the school washroom and was startled in those first moments. Then I remembered I was supposed to be looking forward to this, although I wasn't really, and that my mother had warned me to make sure I was ready — so I wouldn't be embarrassed.

"Oh," said Emily who knew all about things womanly and had recommended Tampons, "You've finally got the curse." Emily had breasts already too — large ones — and boys called her every day on the phone. She was fourteen. I was only thirteen and had diddly-squat, except my stupid, little, flatulent brother, Greg, whose main job in his life was to make mine miserable.

He'd been exploring my backpack and discovered a box of Emily's recommendations. "What are these?" he said, pulling one apart, "firecrackers? It's got a fuse."

I clobbered him as best I could — till Mom broke us apart — then phoned Emily for some moral support.

Emily was what my mother called a bad influence and she probably was. But what did I care, my dad was going to die because he had a heart attack and you never knew when he'd have another. He didn't do anything about it. He still smoked and drank and didn't exercise, which even at my tender age, I knew was bad for you. I had read all about it in those pamphlets that stood waiting for you to peruse in the doctor's office. It was as though this was supposed to take your mind off your earache and sore throat or whatever, and I suppose it worked — I don't know if we studied this in health class, I seldom paid attention there. I read about how you needed to exercise your unhealthy heart and needed to change your unhealthy diet. My mother seemed to be trying to kill him with food. She never served meat and potatoes only, it was meat and potatoes with gravy, sour cream and butter, followed by a dessert of apple pie heaped with ice-cream, not one scoop but three. She was trying to choke his arteries with cholesterol.

Cholesterol was evil. The pamphlets were very clear about this.

So I stopped eating for him. If my dad was going to die, it was not for lack of my being a good example.

And then, Emily introduced me to Brad.

He took my hand and kissed it.

I died.

Well that's what I told Emily, "I died when he kissed me."

"You'll get used to it," she said.

I didn't know if she meant the kissing or the dying, or how she would know. She was actually right on both counts, but at the time it was all brand new.

Brad kissed me and touched me, gently like, what did the poet say? Like moth murmurs at night, and I liked it when he did. Mind you, when I was thirteen I had no idea about murmuring moths, but knew what I liked.

Brad was a bad influence but he was a good hockey player and hung out at the rink where Emily, and now I, hung out too. He was older than both of us, and why he preferred me over Emily, I can only guess. My legs? My hair? It wasn't my breasts — that's for sure.

Perhaps it was my father's credit card.

I had taken Dad's card with the best of intentions. I was going to purchase a fitness club membership for him, so that he might get some exercise, so that he would become fit and wouldn't die. And I made the purchase at Foley's Gym. I bought him a four-month "trial" membership for $375.00. I thought it a small price to pay for my father's life.

Brad thought it was a wonderful idea.

"You have his credit card?"

"Yeah."

"And you bought a membership for him so he will live longer."

"Yeah, of course. I love my dad. I don't want him to die."

"So you don't want to bug him, huh?"

"No, why would I want to bug my dad?"

"Well I mean, for money or something, right?

"No, of course not."

"That's why you're using the credit card — so you don't have to bug him for money."

"Yes, exactly. Right." I was getting exasperated by his relentless logic but not seeing where it was leading.

"So if YOU want money, you wouldn't want to bug him for it."

"No, I wouldn't. I don't. He never gives it to me anyway!"

"Well then we can use the credit card to get some money so you don't have to bug him for it. And you'll be happy and he'll be happy."

At the time, this seemed totally, completely logical to me and I let him convince me to use the card to buy a pair of car tires because he knew where he could sell them for cash. So I bought the tires with my father's card, and together Brad and I rolled them down 22nd Street till we came to the corner of Avenue T.

"Wait here," Brad said.

I waited.

First an old guy in a car stopped. He leaned through the passenger window and asked if I wanted a ride. I shook my head no. He took out his wallet and slapped it on the dashboard. It was bulgy. I didn't have the vaguest notion of what he was getting at but he looked at me like this meant something. Again, I shook my head no. He shook his head and rolled off in a cloud of dust. Then a young guy in a truck pulled up.

"Hey Honey, you want to party? I got some beer."

"No," I said.

"What do you mean 'no?' I got paid last night."

"I'm waiting for my boyfriend." Having a boyfriend made me feel important. And safe.

"Well then fuck you, you dumb bitch," he said and peeled off.

Eventually Brad showed up with $60 and we went to the Dairy Queen. I told him about the men and he said they were "johns," and I could have made some money if I went with them.

"My parents said not to get into cars with strangers," I said.

"They hardly even touch you," he said.

"I was waiting for you," I said.

"Oh," he said.

We bought hamburgers and Peanut Buster Parfaits. I ate them. They were perfect, and it was perfect love, especially when Brad pressed his hard body against me in the alley, and I was smothered in moth wings dark and dusky.

On Father's Day, I gave my dad the membership to the Foley's Gym. He smiled and thanked me. Then Mom asked how I paid for it.

"Credit card," I said.

"Whose?" Mom asked, as if she couldn't figure it out.

"Dad's," I said.

She immediately got on the phone and cancelled it, ordering a full refund, threatening to sue if they didn't give it, and demanding to know how and why they'd let a thirteen-year-old child make such a purchase.

They didn't find out about the tires till two weeks after, when Dad got his credit card statement. Of course I claimed innocence and by the time I told the truth, the police were involved and the credit card company had fraud charges rolling. I had tried to protect Brad, but Greg, my ever watchful, annoying and farting little brother, had seen Brad and I rolling the tires down the street.

This was not Brad's first offence. The police took him to Wilbur Hall. I got twenty hours of volunteer work at the Crisis Nursery.

But I'm getting ahead of myself.

Between all this was summer.

When I said my parents had nothing in common, that is not precisely true: they had the canoe — it was what they fought over most. Actually, it was a series of canoes. First it was the green canoe. Then it somehow became a pock-marked orange canoe that he had acquired, he said, in a trade. He painted the orange canoe red. Whenever Dad loaded the red canoe onto the top of the car, we knew there'd be a fight. It would be one that Dad always won.

Despite not fitting any stereotype in Guns and Reels — no beefy jaw, no steely eyes — fishing was a passion for Dad. He was as devoted to it as he was to his job, although I don't comprehend how one could be devoted to being a loans officer at the Credit Union. Mom was a TA — a "teacher associate" — and contributed almost as much income into our home as Dad. We weren't rich, but we weren't poor either. We were comfortable, comfort being the operative word here — the desired state of being, the Nirvana to be striven for. And we had achieved it.

So why someone would chose to be uncomfortable was beyond Mom. She loathed the outdoors. She hated the mosquitoes, black flies, tree roots, twigs, sand, smoke and the perpetual state of dampness that comes with fishing and camping in northern Saskatchewan. Anytime she saw Dad loading the canoe, it meant either she was being abandoned, (and Dad was thwarting his domestic responsibilities of cutting the lawn and mending the fence, etc.) or she would force herself to join him and drench herself in misery and take the rest of us with her. Which of course, she sometimes did, just for spite.

I must admit here that I share this outdoor-hating trait with my mother. I hated it then, every minute of it, and still do now. I'm not proud of it, but it's a simple fact. However, back then, dragged out into the wilderness, in the grey cold drizzle of mid-July, undergoing my second ever visit by the Red Rag Lady, pining desperately for my lost love and his mothy touch, suffering not only the onslaughts of the Great Outdoors but the taunts of my stupid little brother as well, I was in absolute hell. My mother, my brother and I together, the three of us impounded inside the camper.

Greg and I carped at each other. Between farts, Greg was trying to walk on the ceiling, or so it seemed. While lying on his back, he was throwing a pillow up in the air and trying to catch it with his feet. I was attempting to fix an earring Brad had given me. It was a little tiny "gold" hockey stick with a puck attached to a little tiny "gold" chain. The puck had come off.

Mom was trying to make the best of a bad situation. She had been doing a crossword puzzle and listening to some endless, indecipherable voices droning over a thin, crackling radio.

Dad, of course, was in heaven. He was off fishing in his red canoe.

I flung the hockey stick and puck at Greg. Greg howled.

Mom snarled at us. "Stop, you two! Get a book! Read, or something!"

"How can I read with HIM FARTING every ten seconds!" Which is what Greg had been doing, although perhaps not that often. It just seemed that way.

"Greg, stop farting!" Mom commanded.

"If I don't fart, I'll explode," Greg explained. He was stating a scientific fact. It's funny in retrospect, but at the time he was serious. We were all serious.

"I'm going for a walk!" I huffed.

"You can't go for a walk, it's raining!" Mom would never have gone for a walk in the rain.

"So, it's raining. It's better than dying of suffocation here with YOU," I said pointedly in that obnoxious way that thirteen-year-old girls have of being pointedly obnoxious.

I stepped out of the camper, then promptly, as I was putting my arms through the sleeves on my rain jacket, I stubbed my toe on a beer bottle Dad had left sprawling on the ground. Furious, I picked it up and hurled it into the bush.

Glass shattered.

For a moment, I felt guilt. We were camping in virtual marsh. How had the bottle found a rock? It didn't matter. I abandoned my brief moment of remorse. I was going to have my huffy walk in the rain, think of Brad and his hard body and how totally unfair life was, get all wet, bleed between my legs, and be as completely and totally miserable as I possibly could.

"Hey! Wait!" It was Greg, stomping barefoot after me. "Mom said I had to go along."

"No! You are not coming with me!" Misery did not want company, at least not this company. "I want to be alone."

"She said . . . "

"I don't care what she said!" I screamed. "I'm having my period and I want to be alone!" I doubt he knew exactly what that meant, but it scared him off sufficiently to put some space between us. I didn't care if he followed me — at a distance — just as long as he didn't get within my vision. I could still hear him crashing along behind me.

Somewhere the sun shone. Somewhere people were happy. Somewhere. Not here.

Suddenly there was a cry. "Aaah-aah!" It was thin and high, like a little girl's voice but I knew it was Greg even though I had never heard him make a sound like it before. My first thought was "bears!" I knew there were bears around, and immediately wondered if running towards Greg's cries was the right thing to do, but I kept on running — thrashing really — towards them anyway.

When I got there, Greg was sitting on a rock. At the base of the rock were shards of glass. And red. Lots of red.

"I feel sweaty," said Greg.

"Just be calm," I said.

Blood was soaking his pant leg. I pulled the pant up. Blood spurted from him in regular throbs. Greg had somehow slashed his foot from the arch to the ankle.

"I thought it was a twig poking at me," he said.

Greg watched it as though it was a pretty red fountain. I knew enough to stop it by applying pressure.

"We need something to tie your leg with," I said. "Here, hold your foot here," I made him put his finger on the artery. I used one of the glass shards to start a tear in his pants. I wanted to cut a strip to wrap the gaping wound. I wasn't strong enough, but did manage to rip his pants from the hip to the ankle. I removed his belt and his pants promptly fell to the ground.

"My pants!" said Greg.

"Take them right off," I said.

Greg released the pressure on his foot, stood and tried to stomp out of his pants. They flopped around, blood splashing everywhere. I tugged at the bottom, blood mingled with rain. "Sit!" I commanded.

Poor Greg sat on the rock in his underwear, shivering and whimpering, while I tied his pants around his foot as best as I could. "Keep putting pressure on it." I said. Pressure on the wound was important. It was another thing I'd learned from those pamphlets in the doctor's office.

An unmistakable odour filled the wet air.

"Greg? Did you just fart?"

"I can't help it," he said.

"You're incredible," I said. I hugged him then placed my jacket over his shoulders. "I'll go get Mom."

Greg had grown noticeably paler in the few minutes it took for Mom and I to return. "I'm tired," he said. A thin dull film wrapped his eyes. His white, knobby-kneed legs stood out against his crimson foot. "Oh my God!" Mom said. "Oh my God!" Then quickly gathered Greg into her arms. "I'm taking him to the hospital. Right now. Go tell your dad." She half-trotted towards our campsite. To where the car was parked.

I stood in the rain and watched till she was out of sight. I heard car doors slam. I heard the car drive off. With my rain jacket in it. I wondered if Greg would bleed to death.

I strode along the shore, scanning out onto the water from where Dad had set off with the canoe. There was no sign of human life.

The lake was not that big and there were no major bays or inlets that I knew of — which didn't mean there weren't any. Dad could just as easily have been casting from onshore somewhere.

A great blue heron appeared, flying low from behind a small point of land. I guessed that Dad was there, having scared the bird from its hunting grounds. I could no longer walk on the shore because the bush was too thick. So I marched in the water, sliding over the stones, fighting to stay upright. My feet hurt.

As I rounded the point, it was like entering another world: the skies turned a brilliant orange sending the birds to chatter and flit about as though it were dawn, and there was the canoe pulled up on shore maybe two hundred metres away. But no sign of Dad. I immediately thought he's had another heart attack.

I called. There was no answer, no sign of life around the canoe and no one emerging from the bush. Perhaps he'd gone ashore to relieve himself. Then I noticed something in the water. Maybe a duck or gull. Or muskrat. It disappeared beneath the water for a few moments then rose, head and shoulders splashing. It was Dad! I called again and waved. He didn't seem to hear. I hoped he would get in the canoe and come to me. I didn't want to have to wade all the way to him. I called yet again. He still ignored me. I must have sounded like a bird of some sort because I was sure my voice carried across the water. Why else would he have ignored me?

Then he waved. And waved. And waved some more.

It was as though he was trying to tell me something. I had no idea what. He stood there for a time, his head and shoulders above the water. Then he turned and began to march ashore and I saw what he'd been trying to signal: for me to turn around.

Dad was naked. I could see quite clearly his white sagging bum atop his skinny legs. Although I was spared frontal nudity, I saw my dad as I'd never seen him before, as a sexual being — someone who went swimming in the nude when he was alone and thought no one would see, especially his thirteen-year-old daughter.

It wasn't too long before Dad (fully dressed) paddled to meet me. I blurted out what had happened to Greg even before climbing into the canoe. Dad was silent. He handed me a life jacket and I put it on, glad for the warmth it gave. He began paddling, but rather than heading towards our camp, he started in the opposite direction.

"Where are you going?" I asked.

"There's a hole this way I want to try."

"We have to go back to the camper," I said.

"Why? They'll be gone for hours yet. There's nothing we can do but wait," he said.

"It doesn't have anything to do with them. I don't have any tampons with me."

"Oh," he said. "I see. Are we in a big hurry, or do we just have to get back before too long?"

"Before too long," I said, not wanting to wreck his entire day. "I'm wet and cold too."

"Don't whine like your mother," he said.

I didn't like being compared to my mother.

He kept paddling in the direction he had begun and I sat in the front of the canoe facing him. I felt silly not being able to do anything. The silence was awkward and empty. I tried to fill it.

"Did you catch anything?"

"No," he said. He paddled as though I wasn't there. This irked me.

"Greg might bleed to death," I said, raising the stakes.

"He'll be okay," was all he said. I knew he'd probably be okay too — as long as he kept pressure on it, the bleeding would eventually stop. That's what the pamphlet said. But there was no pamphlet that told you how to talk to your father, or get him to stop looking through you, to make him look you in the eye.

"Some men tried to pick me up," I said.

"What?" He not only looked at me, he stopped paddling too. "When?"

"When I was waiting for Brad — that time with the tires."

"You never told us that before."

"I didn't think it was important."

"What did they look like?"

"The guy in the car was old. The guy in the truck was young."

"Did you get their licence plate numbers?"

"No."

"Of course not. How foolish of me." He was being sarcastic. He began paddling again, righting the canoe to the direction he wanted to go. "You know what they wanted, don't you?"

"Sex. They were 'johns,'" I said.

"Where do you learn all this? Where are you getting this from?" he asked.

I knew that if I said Brad, he'd be provoked. Or provoked in a way that I didn't want him to be. So I said Emily.

"You kids know more than you should," he said.

"Yeah, like seeing your dad naked," I said. This was how I wanted to provoke him.

"That was an accident." With that, he intended to dismiss this discussion. It was well out of his comfort zone.

What was the accident? That I'd seem him, or that he'd been swimming nude? And how did you define accident? Greg's foot, now that was an accident, no one would argue about it, but was the bottle hitting a rock? Was Dad's leaving it lying on the ground where I could stub my toe then pick it up and throw it? Was that an accident? How about his heart attack? An accident? If you thought about it, everything had a cause. Everything had an explanation. You just had to find out what it was.

There was no such thing as an accident.

Dad had put the paddle in the canoe, and while he organized his rod and reel, we drifted. After the rain and with the clearing skies, there was only a breath of a breeze. True to form, Dad placed a large red spoon on the end of his line.

"There's pickerel down there, I know there is."

The line from his rod hissed followed by the distant *ker-PLUNK* of his spoon. He let it settle for a few moments then began reeling.

"I'm glad you were swimming though, I mean, like getting exercise."

"I wasn't swimming for exercise, I was trying to retrieve a lure I lost."

"Oh." I must have sounded disappointed. I wasn't though. I was very annoyed.

"It was my favourite. I couldn't find it." He cast again and began reeling the line in. "Don't worry Sweety, I'm going to live for a while yet." He never called me "Sweety" unless he was drunk, although he used to call me that all the time when I was much younger. "My little girl has got to start eating more," he said.

"You're stupid! You're just so stupid! You're dying! And I'm not 'Sweety', and I'm not your little girl! I'm a woman having my period!" I screamed at him.

He just didn't get it. He didn't seem to hear. He was still reeling in his line. The rod was bent.

"I've got something," he said.

I was seeing red, and all he could think about was his stupid fish.

"It's maybe a snag, except it's moving. Maybe a log." He wasn't explaining to me, he was just thinking out loud. "What the hell is it?" He kept reeling and as he reeled, he was hauling the canoe in the direction of whatever it was he'd snagged.

"Who cares!" I grabbed his tackle box and threw it over the side, almost dumping the canoe as I did so.

"Careful!" he said. "You don't want to tip this. I have a heart condition you know." He smiled. The box was tied to the gunwale and wouldn't go far, even if it sank.

Suddenly I saw my dad for the first time — a complete and utter stranger.

Gradually, slowly, a dark form began to emerge from the water's depths. It was a log — two logs — but broader.

"Oh, my God," Dad murmured. "Turn around," he said to me.

I stared.

"Turn around!" he yelled.

By then I could see it was a body. A human body. Dad had snagged it by the boot. A red bandanna was tied around its ankle, like the kind people tie around dogs' necks to make them look cute. A tangle of rope bound the body's hands behind its back. I couldn't take my eyes off it regardless of what my dad told me to do.

When I finally turned away, I could not look my dad in the eye. It was as though this cold dead thing he dragged from the green water, with its hands tied, was him.

Dad held on for another twelve years but lived eleven of them alone. He never stopped fishing though but sold the red canoe when Mom left him. She took Greg and I with her.

Brad vanished from my life and played professional hockey for a time. I heard he died in a house trailer in Florida. Guns were involved. Drugs.

Greg survived, but the glass from the broken bottle had cut a tendon and left him with a limp. If he still farts, he is much more discreet about it. We get along well these days and he's the one who fishes.

"Remember the time you and Dad found that body?" he says almost every time he prepares for one of his trips.

"Yes," I say, "how could I forget." It was that moment when a door opened, then slammed shut and remained that way.

We never found out anything about the body, although a brief article appearing in the Star Phoenix at the time said no foul play was suspected.

It was an accident.

THE WITCH'S DAUGHTERS

When Robin was very young, his mother would read him fairy tales before he went to bed, and make sure he drank his nightly glass of milk. He believed every word of the tales but hated his milk. Later, Robin grew to tolerate milk, but he no longer believed in fairy tales; nevertheless, certain images hung on. For example, he suspected a neighbour woman might be a witch.

Both of the witch's houses across the street from Robin's were unpainted, dark and foreboding. A path that ran between them gave the distinct impression it was used often. However, this was unlikely given that the smaller of the two houses was unoccupied — not then, and not in the recent past. If you peeked through the dusty cobwebbed windows — and Robin did peek through them, you could see the dull, faded greens and yellows of the walls and the bare planked floors — lighter in the centre where carpets or linoleum once lay.

The yard was a tumble of plants and overgrown grasses the names of which Robin did not know. Nonetheless, he did recognize the sparrows, finches and warblers that sought refuge in the foliage, as well as the bright red flowers that grew in bunches on the west and south sides of the house — poppies

— oodles of them. Robin loved to shake their pods after the petals had left and sprinkle the black seeds onto his tongue.

Surrounding the poppies on three sides of the yard were tall, overgrown caragana hedges that never let enough light onto the grasses beneath. The grass grew long and spindly, and kept the ground cool and dry. This greenery made a natural blind — great for spying from while hiding anyone within — and slightly dangerous because it was inside the yard.

This was where Robin hid when he saw the witch's daughters, or even — on occasion — the witch herself, emerge from the larger house at the other end of the path.

Even though Robin was only eleven years old that summer, he knew that the sisters were exceptionally beautiful, that they could not hide their beauty from the dry shade of the tall caraganas nor the young eyes that gazed from there. And he knew they were sisters because they looked and moved alike. It puzzled him that such beautiful creatures could have a mother who was so ugly. He wondered if the old witch was really their mother or if they were strange fairy tale prisoners — or maybe cursed princesses — instead.

Robin watched from his vantage beneath the caragana as the sisters worked in their garden, filled with thick, black loam and parades of greenery all standing at attention. The sisters hoed between the rows, then pulled with their long fingers the weeds that grew in among the plants. One sister was taller than the other and he could not tell if she was older or younger. She was the one who laughed more, and who sometimes played tricks on the smaller. Her tricks were simple, like putting a leaf on the other's shoulder from behind her back, then pointing and saying, "Worm! Worm!" and laughing at the dance her smaller sister undertook to rid the leaf.

One day the tall sister walked up the path towards the small house near where Robin lay hidden. He held his breath hoping to see her go inside. Instead, she turned towards the poppies and when in their midst, tore their heads off and gathered them among the folds of her great dark skirt.

She drew closer and closer to Robin but her back was to him. Suddenly, she turned and looked right into his eyes as though she had known he had been there all along. Then she smiled at him like it was their little joke — a secret between them — before she turned again and walked away, the autumn leaves swirling about her skirts as she passed among them.

Winter came, and Robin forgot about the witch's daughters, and the path between the two houses.

He concentrated on hockey instead.

Robin wasn't the most skilled player to lace on a pair of skates, and he would have been more so if it wasn't for his tendency to stand and watch the game. It wasn't that he was lazy, he just enjoyed being close to the action — not necessarily in it. However, this tendency did contribute to his single talent as a player. When the puck came to him, which it did with some frequency, he got rid of it with amazing speed and accuracy.

He was a gifted passer of the puck.

The person to whom he most often passed was the star of the team, Kyle Roberts. Kyle and Robin became best friends on and off the ice even though Kyle teased him about his name like everybody else. He hated the name. There was a Robin at school who was a girl except she spelt hers with a "y" instead of an "i." Still, Kyle was the brother Robin never had, and Robin was a relief away from the other six brothers that Kyle did have — three older and three younger.

Robin couldn't wait to show Kyle the beautiful witches that lived across from him. They would hide together under the caraganas and watch to see if they did any magic in their yard, in the garden or on the mysterious path that led from one house to the other.

When the birds finally returned with spring, Kyle ventured with Robin into the witch's yard.

"Keep low!" said Robin.

As they settled beneath the caraganas amid the grasses, a pair of startled sparrows fluttered up and startled them in return. They soon resumed their watch.

"Well, where are they?"

"They're not always here, just sometimes. Want to look in the window?" It beckoned from the small house nearby.

"Nah, I'd rather go through it."

"Through it? You mean, go inside?" Robin hadn't ever considered entering the house. The thought simultaneously thrilled and terrified him. What if they got caught? Or worse, what if the house held some terrible dark secret, something that might devour or destroy them? Not to mention the logistics of gaining entry. "How?"

"You get a rock, Robin, and you put it through the window."

The answer was so simple, so straightforward — like putting the puck in the net, if that was your talent and you had a puck. Or a rock.

"There are no rocks here." It was true. The witch's yards were rock-free. Or had been.

"Yeah? What do you call those?" And there, in the middle of the path that spanned the two yards, rose a mound of stones the size of a doghouse. Aside from that, nothing else had changed — or nothing discernable.

"I wonder where they came from?"

"What do you mean?" asked Kyle.

"Well they weren't here last year."

"Maybe something's buried there. Like a body. Or a treasure. You wait here, I'll go get one." With that, Kyle sprinted to the pile.

He's serious, thought Robin, he's going to break a window. Peeking through a window might be illegal, but there was no doubt about breaking a window. THAT was vandalism. It would make him a vandal, an outlaw.

Seconds later, Kyle returned, hefting a stone in his hand. "Which one do you want to do? This one?" He indicated the near window.

"I don't want to do any of them."

"Oh come on, do you want to see the inside or don't you?"

"I want to see inside, but . . . "

The sound of collapsing glass interrupted his answer. Kyle broke away the remaining shards with the heel of his palm, careful not to cut himself. He hoisted himself inside. "Come on!" he said, then disappeared within the house.

Robin was half-in, half-out — his toes kicking the clapboard siding, his head straining through the window frame — when a door opened in the larger house. He couldn't see this. But Kyle could.

"Hurry!" said Kyle, yanking Robin by the shoulders, tumbling him onto the dusty floor. Then, with their eyes peering above the window ledge they watched two dark figures emerge from the house. The sisters. They started up the path. The shorter one carried a basket and stopped at a clothesline strung from their house to a pole in the back. She began hanging laundry. The taller sister continued along the path. She carefully stepped around the stone pile and strolled out of their vision to the back of the small house.

Robin and Kyle heard a key being inserted into the padlock at the back door, then a rattle as it was loosed. The door creaked open, and footsteps scuffled inside..

"Hide!" said Kyle.

"Hide where?" said Robin who recognized a bad situation when he saw one.

They scrambled into a corner of the room, which had likely been a bedroom. It was small and the furthest from the back door. A confused clattering emanated from the rear that sounded like tin cans tumbling down a garbage chute, followed by silence — followed by intermittent thumping.

Robin and Kyle looked at each other.

Then, before they had a chance to breathe twice and collect their thoughts, a sparrow flew in through the broken window. It swooped once around the room, careened through the doorway and disappeared from sight. But not from sound. The clattering they heard earlier began again but this time was mixed with a high shriek.

Robin ran towards the noise.

First he saw the bird, alighted upon an old cast iron kitchen stove, then the tall girl cowering in a corner amid a heap of tin cans which had spilled from a burlap sack.

"Get rid of it," she said.

Robin picked up the sack from the floor, emptied it of the remaining cans and crept towards the terrified sparrow. Just as he was about to spread the sack over it, the bird flew up against the window, fluttering and battering itself against it. Stunned, it settled on the floor.

"Get it! Get it!" said the girl.

Robin spread the sack over it and gently picked it up. He could barely feel the bird inside the coarse, raw burlap. He returned to the bedroom and carefully unfolded the sack at the window, setting the bird free.

It flew into the daylight beyond.

Turning back into the room, Robin realized he was alone, that Kyle had fled out the window sometime ahead of the bird. Robin wondered if he should follow too and attempt an escape. He did not hear the tall sister approach behind him.

"Thank you," she said, "I'm terrified of birds."

Then she noticed the broken window. She didn't say anything, she just looked at Robin.

"I did it," Robin said, and started gathering up shards of glass and placing them on the burlap.

The tall sister stepped further into the small room and bent over to pick up the large stone that Kyle had sent through the pane. "My mother will be angry," she said.

"Don't tell her," Robin pleaded. "I'll pay for it."

"Where will you get the money?" She turned the rock over in her hand.

"I have some. And my friend Kyle. He'll have some too." This was true. Kyle always seemed to have money. And he knew Kyle would owe him big time. But whether he would get any from him would be another matter, as was how you would actually go about fixing a window. It was too much. He didn't want to think about it.

The tall girl studied him. He felt her deep, dark eyes peering right inside his soul. Robin was suddenly afraid she might see things he didn't even know were there.

"I'll help you. I'll help around," he blurted. He was worried about what she might do with the rock in her hand.

"I know you, don't I."

"I don't think so."

"You thought you were hiding from my sister and I when we worked in the garden last year."

She had known all along — they both had known. He might as well introduce himself.

"My name's Robin."

"I'm Julia." She placed the rock in her left hand and extended her right towards Robin. "I've never met a bird before," she smiled.

Robin's hand tingled when she touched him. She led him to the back porch where a thousand tin cans lay. They were old soup or vegetable cans — big ones — open at both ends, strewn among various rakes, hoes and other garden tools.

"The cans," she said loading Robin's arms full of them, "are to protect the plants."

"What kind of plants?"

"Herbs mostly."

Outside, walking along the path, Julia stopped at the pile to carefully replace the stone that had shattered the window. "These shouldn't be moved," she said. "Otherwise bad things might happen. They're Carla's."

Robin didn't know who Carla was, or if it was she or the stones that made bad things happen.

The other sister, who had since finished hanging laundry, shovelled heaps of compost onto a small area of garden.

"Carla!" Julia called, "This is Robin. He's helping."

Carla barely looked up from her task. "Put them here," she said referring to the cans Robin carried.

"For the hellebore?" asked Julia.

"Yes," said Carla. "And the Wort."

"What's hellebore?" ask Robin.

"A plant," said Carla.

"It has red sap," said Julia. "It looks like blood. If you step on it after sunset, a fairy-house will appear and take you away. You plant it next to the Saint John's Wort for balance."

"It keeps the demons away," said Carla.

"Demons?"

"Demons sometimes join the fairies and their hounds on the wild hunt. It usually means death is near."

When Robin met Kyle later that week, he told him of the sisters' weird plants and what they said about the stones. He told him of the wild hunt, of the demons and death. He'd mostly forgotten the names of the plants — hell something and saint something — one seemed to be good, the other bad. And although he didn't tell Kyle, he remembered the names of the sisters.

"They're witches for sure," said Kyle. "And you're working for them?"

"I got to pay for the window somehow. You should actually be working for them because you broke the window." Robin hoped Kyle might take the hint and fork over some cash.

But Kyle wasn't listening. "What do you suppose is under that pile?"

"What pile?"

"That pile of stones. It must be covering something — hiding something. Maybe a treasure. Or a body. We got to look."

"I told you, no one's supposed to touch them. Bad things might happen."

"They're just trying to scare you — to keep you away from the treasure. I'll get my brother's flashlight. He's got one that's real powerful."

"But I'm working for them. I don't think it's a good idea. Besides, it's theirs — not ours."

"It's a pile of stones. Nobody owns a pile of stones. Stones belong to everybody — like air."

"Yeah but . . ."

"But what?"

"It's their yard and their path. We would be trespassing."

"No we're not — you work for them! How can you trespass on a place where you work?"

Kyle's logic was impeccable. There was no point in arguing. But it was only fair to point out the danger.

"Just make sure you don't step on any of those hell plants."

"I don't believe in any of that crap. What is a fairy house anyway? A place where fairies hang out?" Kyle made a limp wrist in mockery. "And how can a house take you away?"

"Maybe she meant horse."

"Anyway, there's no such thing as fairies — not that kind anyway."

"Yeah? What about demons?"

"Demons either. They said that to keep you from the stones."

Maybe this was true. All that week when he'd been helping the sisters after school, it seemed they went out of their ways to avoid the pile. Indeed, the path upon which the stones had been set, now swerved in a large arc around them. "Tell your mom you're staying at my place. We'll go after dark."

"It'll almost be midnight then."

"So?"

"That's when the . . . " Robin hesitated. He wanted to say "ghosts" but that sounded like he might be afraid, so he chose a word that wasn't quite so scary. " . . . when the spirits come out," he finished.

"Don't be an idiot," said Kyle.

Robin's mother was pleased to let him tent at his friend's on a Friday night. She said it would save her finding a sitter because she needed to get out of the house herself. They would both be happy.

It was exceptionally warm and muggy for late May. If there was a moon, it hid behind a heavy drape of clouds.

"I thought you said your brother's flashlight was good?"

"I'm just saving the battery for when we need it at the pile."

"We have to see where we're going!"

"Don't be such a wuss."

As they passed beyond the caraganas into the yard, they widened their eyes trying to see in the increased darkness — where the street lights didn't reach.

"This way," Robin whispered.

Above the back porch door of the witch's house, a naked bulb hung amid small eccentric orbits of moths and gnats. It was so quiet you could hear them clicking against the light bulb. It also made the shadows larger and darker than they already were.

"It should be right around here." Robin began lifting his feet higher and walking slower to avoid stumbling.

"Nah, it's . . . " Kyle didn't finish his sentence. There was a muffled thump, the shock of rocks grinding together, then the momentary clatter of plastic on a hard surface.

Robin froze. "Kyle? . . . Kyle where are you?" He peered into the black. Then, almost at his feet, he could make out the vague outline of Kyle's brother's flashlight. He bent down, and turned it on. It offered a dirty, dim beam — enough to see Kyle stretched out on the pile of stones. "Kyle! Are you okay?"

Kyle didn't stir.

Moving the feeble light onto Kyle's face, Robin could see the dark outlines of blood oozing from his friend's forehead. He bent close to Kyle's cheek to see if he was still breathing. He was. His mouth was slightly open. A mosquito landed on his lip. Robin brushed it away.

A cold horror settled on Robin. He needed help. Home was not an option. He knew what he had to do.

He bounded across the yard, kicking cans along the way. He knew he was trampling the hell plants but there was nothing he could do about it. He banged on the door below the bare light bulb. There was no answer. He banged harder and shouted, "Hey! Hello!"

Just as he turned away from the door, looking to see other lights in the neighbourhood where he might try to raise help, the door behind him opened.

"Yes?"

He turned, and there she stood, the old witch herself. Her face hid deep within the shadows of the long, grey hair.

Robin's voice stuck his throat.

"Who's there?" A young female voice rose from within the house. Its owner tucked her head out the door around her mother's shoulder. Julia.

"Robin! What are you doing here?" She stepped in front of her mother.

"My friend. He's over there, hurt." Robin waved generally into the darkness behind him. "We need to call 9-1-1."

Julia looked at her mother.

"We don't have a phone," the old woman said.

Within moments, all four were at Kyle's side. Julia placed a moist cloth on Kyle's head. Carla took his hand and massaged its palm. The old lady pulled a vial from within her nightclothes, unstopped it, and held it briefly beneath Kyle's nose. He stirred immediately.

"Kyle! Are you okay?"

He looked up at the dark shadows around him.

"I have just been to the most amazing place," he said. Then he spat a large white worm from his mouth.

"Larva," said the old woman. She pinched it between her fingers and walked away. Her daughters followed.

The dim light of the flashlight barely reached the ground as the boys made their way back to Kyle's backyard. It was after midnight now.

"You should have seen it!" Kyle exclaimed. "It was amazing: this great big cave that was lit by, like, a million candles. And there was this huge table loaded with all kinds of food — roast turkeys, and pigs, and roasts, and mounds of apples with cakes and pies and mugs of drink. All this was laid out for these shiny white knights and their squires who were eating and listening to this music, mostly trumpets. Well not just trumpets, but drums too . . . "

Kyle went on, but none of it made any sense to Robin.

The next day, Robin had a hard time explaining the blood on his sneakers to his mother.

Over time, a shadow grew on Kyle; he became distracted and vague. When he smiled, Robin wondered if he was smiling at him, or at someone just beyond. Robin became uncomfortable around him and avoided him at school.

He never crossed the street again to hide among the caraganas.

The next winter, he played hockey, passing and receiving the puck as well as ever. Kyle was on the team too, but he was no longer the best player. In fact, he had barely made the team. He seemed to have lost his focus, his drive. Shortly after Christmas, he quietly abandoned the team. Then he changed schools. He became a stranger, soon forgotten by everyone. It was as though he had died.

One day in the following spring, Robin felt compelled to cross the street and venture into the witch's yards. Although the caraganas grew and were filled with birds, the small, weathered house was boarded up, contrasting sharply against the fresh coat of paint that smiled brightly on the larger house. But there was no sign of the witch's daughters. The garden had been overlaid with lawn. Weeds grew on the path that had spanned the two houses.

The stone pile was gone.

TIPPY TANGO

I'm walking to school with my mom, and there it is again, that big black car. Every day, same time, same car driving down Stanley Street. You can't see the driver or if anybody's in it because the windows are dark.

"Who's in that car?" I ask my mom.

"What car?" she says.

"The big black one."

"I didn't see it. Must be a gangster, eh? Or maybe the mayor," she says. I think she's making a joke. She has a little wrinkle of a smile on one end of her mouth.

"If it's a gangster then we should have a dog so he can protect us."

"Tyler, don't start," she says. Her mouth wrinkle goes away. It shows up on her forehead. That means she's going to get mad if I don't shut up.

If I didn't shut up and wanted to make her really mad, I would say, "Dad would get me one, a great big one, who could tow you in a sleigh." But I don't say anything. Dad doesn't live with us any more. I saw him sometimes in the summer and I am supposed to visit at Christmas. When I used to believe in Santa, I asked him for a dog every year but he didn't give me one either — because he's not real. Dogs are real. It's only two more weeks — Dad and Christmas. I think I'd rather stay with Mom, even if she doesn't want a dog. Dad yells sometimes.

"Dogs stink up the house," Mom says. We don't even have a house. We have an apartment. If we had a house, then we would have a backyard. We could have a dog and not stink up the house. It could stink up the backyard. No one would care, as long as you cleaned up the poo. People don't like seeing the poo.

Sometimes I pretend I am a camera, so I take pictures. Cameras don't think, they just see things. I'm supposed to paint pictures with words, that's what Ms. Selsky tells us in school. I'd rather be a camera. It's faster. You don't have to think about what word to use next.

My mom goes to school, too. Ms. Selsky isn't Mom's teacher because we don't go to the same school. My mom goes to nursing school, so she can be a nurse. I go to Saint Christopher school, so I can be a saint (Ha-ha, that's a joke.) But my school is on the way to Mom's school, so she walks me there every day. She walks me home, too, about a kilometre down Stanley Street. I meet her on the corner after school — not at the mission but across the street where the video store is. Sometimes I go in if it's too cold or rainy. Mom's friend Laurie works there and lets me check out which movies I'd like to see as soon as we get a DVD player. But usually I just wait outside and watch the cars and trucks go by.

If I was a camera this is what you'd see. The black car, zooming (click, blur). A church and some stores that sell used furniture (click, click), and some stores that sell nothing because they're closed. They have For Sale and For Rent signs in their windows. (Click, click, click.) We pass a restaurant that always has nobody in it except a lady with circles around her eyes. She's always smoking a cigarette. Every day, same lady. (Click, click.) We pass a butcher store with dead meat hanging. (Click.) We pass a Chinese store with red lanterns and squiggledy writing, and a store that has Adult XXX on it and you can't see through the yellow windows. (Click, click.) We pass a library loaded with books, a drugstore loaded with everything, and the Stanley Street Mission that always has people standing around outside. (Click, click, CLICK.)

"Tyler, don't stare," says Mom.

"I'm not staring," I say.

I'm just looking at the people in front of the mission. If you look too long, that's staring. I'm looking at that old man. He's only got one leg. I don't look at him too long. I'm looking at that old lady. She talking to somebody but nobody's there. She doesn't have any teeth either. Maybe I stare a bit at her. Then I'm looking at that boy. He's big as I am. He looks right back at me like he wants to tell me something but can't. I stop staring even though there's more people to stare at.

We walk a few steps past them before I ask why they're standing around.

"They're waiting for the doors to open," says my mom.

"Open to what?"

"Open the soup kitchen. That's where they eat," she says.

"What do they eat?" I ask.

"Whatever they can get, I guess."

"Dogs?"

"Don't be silly! Where'd you get that idea?'

"Some of my friends said."

"Hot dogs maybe. People donate food, businesses donate food. Don't believe everything your friends tell you."

I don't have too many friends, just Christopher with glasses (not the saint) and Natalie with red hair, because we just moved here last year after Mom moved away from Dad. Christopher said his brother told him they eat dogs at the soup kitchen. Natalie said yuck. How are you supposed to know what to believe? I don't get to ask Mom that because she is still talking.

"Some people can't afford to buy their own food. They're too poor to eat at home. Some of them don't even have a home," says my mom. "They have no place to sleep. They sleep outside in boxes."

"In winter time?"

"Behind buildings, in alleys, yes. And they don't have decent coats or boots either. And often they get sick or freeze. And sometimes they die."

They must be poorer than us.

We have a home. We have food to eat at home. I don't always like it when Mom makes soup with potatoes and carrots in it, but we have it and I have to eat it. I like KD and sometimes I get to make it. We have that lots. With wieners in it too. We have a TV. We have warm beds and warm coats. We have good exercise because we walk a lot. We don't have a car.

And we don't have a dog.

That was yesterday we didn't have a dog. Today we do. He followed us home.

This was how we met.

I was waiting for Mom in front of the video store. I could see a dog across the street at the Stanley Street Mission. No one was there — just the dog, sitting there. He was looking at me. I said, "Here boy!" and he came, just like that. He crossed the street, but waited for the cars to pass. He even looked both ways. "Smart dog!" I thought. Then he came and sat beside me. I patted him.

"You're a smart dog," I said to him. He didn't answer anything back but twitched his eyebrows to let me know he heard. It was funny the way he sat there and waited with me — like he had done it all his life.

Pretty soon Mom came.

"Go on!" she said. "Go away," to the little dog. But he wasn't going anywhere without us. He stepped a few feet away and twitched his eyebrows some more. After following us for a while, he started leading us, like he knew where we were going. He's small and black with a little white diamond on his chest.

He bounces when he walks. He sniffs at everything. Then he diddles a bit on some things. He diddled on the building that has Adult XXX on it. Mom smiled with one side of her mouth. I wished I had a camera for that one. (Click, click.)

"Dogs," she said.

"Can we keep him?" I asked.

"Don't be silly," she said. "We have enough trouble making ends meet. Besides, he'll stink up the house."

"We don't have a house," I said.

"Very funny," she said.

"Well, we don't."

"He'll stink up the apartment then, Mr. Man." When she calls me Mr. Man instead of Tyler, that means shut up for a while. So I wait till some time has passed. I watch the little black dog walking and sniffing.

"When are we going to make ends meet, Mom?"

"When your father pays his support," she says. She looks hard ahead. My dad doesn't always send money like he's supposed to. When he doesn't pay, Mom gets mad. But she doesn't want me to know it.

"I'm sorry," she says, "Maybe we'll make ends meet when I finish my degree."

"Ends of what?"

"Ends of the month, meeting with the ends of your money. There's always more month than money."

"So when we make ends meet, then can I have a dog?"

"We'll see," she says.

I hate when she says that. "We'll see" usually always means "no." I'm thinking about this while we're walking, and how we could have a house and a backyard if those ends were meeting. My friend Natalie doesn't have a backyard either. She has a cat. Her mom named it Mork. She says it's from another planet because it sleeps upside down on its back and chases things that aren't there. It can see ghosts. But she and her mom might get kicked out because there's no pets allowed where they live in the apartment building right next door. Pets are allowed where I live. The little black dog is still walking in front of us, walking and sniffing and diddling.

Why do dogs smell other dogs' poo? Weird.

He walks right up to our front door. He doesn't try to follow us inside even though he'd like us to ask. But he can't. He's a dog. He just sits by the door with his eyebrows twitching.

We go up to our apartment. I look out the window to see if the dog is still there. He is. Mom makes supper. It's that soup with potatoes and carrots. How can something that smells so good taste so bad? I do my homework. We eat supper. It takes me a long time to eat because the soup's too hot and also I hate it so much. I finally finish, spilling only a little. I look out the window. Dog is still there. I watch TV. During the commercials, I look again. He's there. This happens all night till Mom says "get ready for bed now." I brush my teeth, put on my pj's. I'm ready for bed. I look out the window one last time.

"Mom, he's still there."

"When he gets bored, he'll leave."

"It's cold out," I say.

"He has a fur coat," she says.

"He's shaking," I say.

"No, he's not," she says.

"Well come and look!"

Mom gets up and comes beside me at the window. "That dumb . . . " Her tongue makes that snick sound off the back of her teeth. "Why doesn't he just go home?"

That's how come I have a dog now because she goes and gets him. She probably saves him from freezing. I can hear them walking up the hallway, Mom clomping in her boots and Dog in his toenails tip-tipping along with his bouncy step. I decide I'll call him Tippy, to go with the sound he makes.

Tippy doesn't bark. He says, "Erf." He sometimes says it like a question, "Erf?" Or sometimes like he's boss, "Erf!" He can say quite a lot with just one word.

"G'night, Tippy," I say.

"Erf," he says.

Mom made me put posters up all over the place advertising that we found a dog. We made ten of them. I put up five in places I thought she'd see. The other five I threw in the dumpster. No one called us. She phoned the SPCA and no one was looking for a small black dog. He doesn't stink up the apartment. He doesn't stink up anything. He smells pretty good; like a dog though, not like a flower. We take him for long walks every night after supper and very short walks every morning before breakfast.

The night walks are more interesting because they're longer and he gets to sniff around. I let him lead the way. His favourite places are the back alley that leads to the graveyard and the graveyard itself. Mom usually stays at home and does her homework. She's glad that I'm out of her hair. I'm glad too.

At first I was scared of going into the graveyard, but Tippy isn't, and if he isn't, why should I be — even if it's dark? There're no ghosts there, or if there are, you can't see them because all the snow is white — same colour as ghosts — see-through white. The only things we see are footprints. They always stop at the same place — a stone that says Edward James Mahon, 1987 – 1997. That's all it says. There's a bird carved on the stone too. A pigeon, I think. Everyday, same prints. They come and go, even after a storm. I don't know anything about Edward James Mahon, except that he died when he was ten.

It's after Christmas now, and I saw my dad for five days. He never yelled, except once when I talked too long on the phone with Mom. Dad has a computer and I played games on it. It was cool. Now I want a computer too. "Dream on," my mom says.

There is lots more snow and colder too. It takes us longer to walk to school. Even though it's colder, there are still lots of people waiting for the doors to open at the Stanley Street

Mission. I don't stare anymore. I just want to hurry by in case I see that boy again. Sometimes I think I do, but it's just me reflecting in the window. Sometimes that black car we see in the morning is parked in front of the mission after school.

"There's that car," I say to mom.

"What car?"

"The one we see in the morning."

"There are lots of cars in the morning, Tyler," she says sort of loud. I can tell I'm not supposed to ask any more questions right now. So I don't.

How come things stay the same for days and days? Nothing changes. Same old boring stuff. Then all at once, a bunch of things happen in a row for no reason that you can think of. Like for days and days it's cloudy, then all of a sudden, it's sunny out.

When Ms. Selsky isn't teaching us how to make pictures with words, she's teaching us Social Sciences and has given us reading assignments — the newspaper. She says the newspaper has "articles" of news that tell the story of our world. The newspaper is pretty boring except for the comics or mini-clips, and it's got mostly ads in it. They should call it the "adspaper." But anyway, I found two things that were interesting. The first was that the Stanley Street Mission is closing because it doesn't have enough money to stay open. The headline was *Mission to Close*. This is how the article started: *After twenty-three years of operation, the Stanley Street Mission is in danger of closing its doors for lack of funding leaving hundreds without regular hot meals. What are those people going to do? Where will they eat?*

The second article wasn't really an article but an ad in the classified section. I would never have read it, but it had a picture above it. Ms. Selsky says a picture is worth a thousand words. I couldn't think of any words for this picture. Except maybe "yikes." It was of a small black dog that looked like Tippy. It read: *Reward for return of small black dog with a white diamond on his chest. Answers to the name, Tango. Please call* . . . and there was a phone number. I cut it out. I cut out the article too.

"What're these holes in the paper?" my mom asked.

"It's for school," I said.

"In the classifieds?"

"It had a picture."

"Of what?"

"A dog, a big white one." I lied. This was a white lie, I think. "Somebody lost it."

"Oh, a husky," she said.

"I think so."

"Let's see," she said.

"I lost it."

"You lost the picture?"

"I accidentally flushed it down the toilet," I said. I didn't yet, but I was going to.

"How could you do that?"

"By accident," I said.

"You don't accidentally flush things down the toilet," she said.

"I'm sorry."

She looked at me with that wrinkle on her forehead and pinched eyes. "Get ready for supper," she said.

I did. We ate tuna casserole with cheese on top. It was good. Tippy sat under the table maybe hoping we'd drop something because he never begs out front. He was a good dog.

On Saturday Mom and I go shopping at Stupid Store. That's what Mom calls it even though it's supposed to be Super Store. We take Tippy with us. I hold him on the leash. He doesn't need one but there is a law that says you must tie your dogs to a leash. We are walking on the sidewalk that goes the opposite way from school. It's sunny but it's pretty cold. Cars on the street make clouds behind them. Sometimes they hide the next car coming. Then suddenly out of a cloud comes the black car we see every morning when we walk to school. It slows as it passes us. It just about stops. It feels like someone is staring. Mom walks faster and I have to run every three or four steps to keep up. Then the car takes off. We start walking normally again.

"How come that car slowed?" I ask my mom.

"What car?" she says.

"The one that was following us, that made you hurry."

"I'm hurrying because I'm cold. You and your black cars," she says.

"Didn't you see the car that was beside us?"

"You have an overactive imagination," she says.

"How come you slowed down when it passed?"

"Because we're stopping here. I have to get a few more things."

"Here" is the drugstore. I go inside but just wait by the door because I hate drugstores. Except the candy section, but Mom never goes there. I watch the grocery bags so nobody takes them. I watch Tippy who is tied to a signpost outside again like he was at Stupid Store. While I'm waiting and watching in the doorway, I read the signs and posters. Things are for sale, like a 4 X 4 truck, a computer for three hundred dollars (where would I get three hundred dollars?) and a box spring and mattress. And yoga is on Tuesday nights, and Weight Watchers is on Thursdays. And a picture of a dog that looks like Tippy. I read the sign.

Lost. Small black dog with a white diamond on his chest. Answers to the name Tango. Reward offered. please call attached number below. On the bottom of the poster a phone number is written on little strips of paper that you can tear one off like the fringes on a coat.

I tear off the whole poster because I don't want my mom to see it. Tippy might be Tango. I put it in my pocket fast.

When we get home, I try out the other name on Tippy.

"Here Tango," I say. He comes to me, wagging his tail. I immediately feel sick in my stomach like somebody has put a heavy thing there.

"What did you call him?" my mom asks.

"Nothing," I say.

"Yes, you did. You called him something else."

"My lips got tangled up," I say. "He came because it was my voice." Maybe this is true. "What are we having for supper?" I ask.

"Are you trying to change the subject?" she asks.

"No," I say.

"Leftovers — tuna casserole," she says.

"Sit Tuna," I say to Tippy. Tippy sits. "See?" I say. "He just listens to my voice. You can call him anything."

"I see, " she says. I can tell by the way she says "I see" that she doesn't believe me a hundred percent.

Tuna casserole, two nights in a row. Not as good tonight.

"What I wouldn't give for a T-bone steak," mom says.

"Is it too expensive?" I ask.

"Come here," she says but doesn't answer my question and gives me a hug instead.

When I take Tippy for his evening walk and we end up at the graveyard as usual, somebody is walking towards us, towards the gravestone that says Edward James Mahon on it. It's too dark to see his face but he's not too big and takes small hurried steps from the other end of the cemetery where the road is. And his car. It looks black. I wonder if it's the same one I see in the mornings. It's not the first time I saw someone at the graveyard, but it's the first time I see somebody from the big black car.

Big surprise when the walking person gets to me and Tippy. He's a she.

"Hello," says the lady, "I wondered when I'd meet you. I see your footprints every day. And what a nice dog!" She bends to pet him. "What's his name?"

"Tippy," I say.

"Erf," says Tippy.

"Tango!" says the lady.

"Erf, erf," says Tippy.

"His name is Tippy," I say.

"He looks just like a dog I knew," she says.

"I had him since he was little," I lie.

"Yes, of course," says the lady. "He can't be Tango. Tango is dead. He's buried right here. With my grandson," says the lady.

"He is?"

"They were both killed in an car accident," she says.

I look at Tippy. His eyebrows get all twitchy, like this is news to him too.

"I got to go now," I say to the lady.

"Nice to meet you," she says. "Take care!"

As we walk back home, I tell Tippy he doesn't look like a ghost to me.

"Erf," he says, which means, "of course I'm not a ghost." He turns to look back at the graveyard — which makes me turn too. And you know what? There's no sign of the lady anymore. Or the black car. She sure is fast.

At school Ms. Selsky wants to know about the articles we saved from the newspaper. Only one other person, Natalie with red hair, picked the same article as me. Ms. Selsky asked how come we picked that article. Me and Natalie said the same reason — where were those people going to eat? Ms. Selsky said we should write a letter to the mayor and ask him. Then the whole class wanted to write a letter to the mayor because they wanted to know where those people were going to eat too. So we made letter-writing teams. Bang, one day, fifteen letters. Just like that.

This was my letter with Natalie. We were a team.

Dear Mr. Mayor

In the paper it said that the Stanley Street Mission was closing because of lack of funding. Where all those people going to eat if it closes? Maybe they can go to your house. They can't come to ours because we live in apartments. Ms. Selsky says it costs more to pave one street than keep the mission open for two years. Is pavement more important than people eating? I hope you can give them money to stay open

Sincerely,
Natalie and Tyler

That's our letter.

Last night Natalie came over to our place with Mork in her arms. Mork is an orange cat the colour of marmalade and is a she cat even though her name doesn't sound like it. Natalie says Mork's fixed, which means she can't have kittens. She needs a place to live because Natalie's mom said she'll have to be put down if they can't find a home for her. "Put down" is a nice way of saying "killed." Mork wasn't too crazy about meeting Tippy. She climbed all over Natalie with her claws out, trying to get away from Tippy who just wanted to play. I guess there are no ghosts at our place because Mork didn't chase anything that wasn't there. She was too busy hanging onto Natalie. I feel sorry for Mork but we can't take her because we have Tippy.

When I meet Mom after school today, she doesn't talk to me. I can tell she's mad about something. After we get home and we take our coats off, she takes a newspaper out of her school bag. I think, "Oh-oh."

"Come here, Mr. Man," she says. "Look what I have. Friday's newspaper. Guess what I find in Friday's newspaper, in the classifieds?"

"An ad," I say.

"For a lost dog, who looks a lot like Tippy." She shakes the paper. "Now I don't care how much you love that dog and want to keep him, I don't want you lying to me. Not now, not then, not ever, never. Is that clear?"

"Yes."

"It better be. Now call that number right now and tell them found a dog that looks like the one in the paper."

Tippy must know we're talking about him because he doesn't say anything and sits under the table with his eyebrows twitching even though he's usually excited to see us when we get home.

I dial the number. At the other end, somebody answers, "Stanley Street Mission," they say.

"Huh?"

"Stanley Street Mission," a man says more slowly this time, even though I heard him the first.

"Did you lose a dog?" I say.

"Oh!" he says real excited, "I had given up. Do you have him?"

"I think so, " I say.

In a few minutes my mom helps make arrangements for us to take Tippy Tango to meet the man at the mission. It has to be next Saturday because we can't take time off school during the day and the man is busy in the evenings.

"But they're closing, why would they want a dog now?" I ask my mom.

"It's somebody's dog. It doesn't necessarily have anything to do with the mission being open or closed," she says.

Saturday comes too fast, so I walk slow down Stanley Street to the mission with Tippy Tango and my mom. Tippy's all bouncy like everything is hunky dory while I feel like a ton of grey, which is the colour of the sky and the snow and just about everything else too. What colour are tears? I guess they're clear but today they would be grey too.

When we get there, two vans and a big black car are parked in front. The vans are pasted with TV logos from different TV stations.

"I wonder what's going on?" says Mom.

Although I walked by the mission a thousand times, I never went in before. It's way smaller than I thought it would be, with three long tables crammed into a space where there should be only two. A big window is cut out of one wall with a counter along the bottom edge and a kitchen on the other side where giant pots steam on stoves. It smells like Mom's soup.

There's a hundred people all around including the lady who talks to herself and the old man with one leg, but mostly people in suits and camera guys with their lights shining bright on some guy who's talking into a microphone.

"Who's that?" I ask my mom.

"The mayor," she says.

"What's he doing here?"

"I have no idea," she says.

"Me and Natalie wrote him a letter," I tell her.

"You what?"

" . . . and the public outcry has been overwhelming," the mayor is saying. "From concerned citizens to school children, letters and messages of all kinds have been pouring in. It's quite clear that this service and the tradition of this service is not one that this community wants to abandon at this time."

"Does the Mohan legacy have anything to do with this decision, your worship?" one of the reporters asks.

"The Mohan legacy was one factor, but not a major deciding factor, yes," says the mayor.

"What's the Mohan legacy?" I ask my mom.

"I don't have the foggiest idea," she says.

"Tango!" Someone yells.

"Erf! Erf!" says Tippy.

"Tango, where have you BEEN?" A man is on his knees hugging Tippy Tango. The man has hair the colour of clouds in the sky, and a pink bald island in the middle of it. He's also got big smiley teeth and a nose like a giant strawberry.

"Actually, he's been with us, " says my mom.

The man on his knees looks up. "Thank you so much. We really missed him around here. He's everybody's friend." Climbing to his feet with Tippy Tango in his arms, he shakes Mom's hand. "I'm Ed," he says, "Edward James."

"How are you Mr. James," she says.

The name Edward James reminds me of something but I don't know what.

"It's a big day around here. We not only secure our funding, we get Tango back." Mr. James nuzzles Tippy, who looks a bit uncomfortable if his twitching eyebrows mean anything.

"We really enjoyed having him, didn't we Tyler?" Mom says.

"Yes," I say. "I'll miss him."

"You can stop by any time and see him," says Mr. James.

It won't be the same, seeing him here and having him lying under the kitchen table or taking him for walks out into the back alley and graveyard where those footprints to that gravestone go.

And then suddenly I remember the name on the gravestone — Edward James Mahon — the same first names as this old guy. And the same last name the mayor talked about — the Mahon legacy.

"What's the Mahon Legacy?" I ask him.

"Well that would be a reference to my sister, Marion, who was instrumental in setting this place up. Probably because of me, because I used to drink a bit and, well, that's not important. At any rate, she died a couple of years ago, her and her grandson, Eddie — named after me. In fact, Tango was Eddie's. He was with them. Tango was the only survivor."

That's not what the lady at the graveyard said. Whoever she was.

"Do you have a car?" I ask.

"A car? Heavens no, I can't afford one. My sister did though. Looked just like the mayor's."

I feel like someone has peeled back the skin from neck and put ice there. I look around the room at all the people. I see the boy. He looks at me. He nods and smiles. Then he goes out the door. I run after him. I go outside. All I can see is a black car pulling off into the grey.

I tell Mom all about the lady and the grave, and the boy I have seen.

"Some things are hard to understand, and you can't explain them," she says. "But some things are easy — like the good you accomplished when you wrote that letter."

"And Natalie," I say. "I think Tippy helped."

We have soup for supper — carrots and potatoes. Dad is late on his payment again. After supper, I want to go for a walk even though Tippy isn't with us any more. I want to remember him. Mom comes with me. She doesn't have to do homework on Saturday night. "This is where Tippy and me used to go," I tell her. In the graveyard the snow is smooth by the gravestones. No one has been here for a while.

"Can we get another dog?" I ask.

"I don't think that would be a good idea right now, " she says.

"Why?"

"It'd be pretty hard for a new dog to live up to Tippy," she says.

It's probably true. "How about a cat? Natalie still has to find a home for Mork," I say.

"A cat," says Mom. She twitches her eyebrows like Tippy used to do.

"It can see ghosts and sleep upside down," I tell her.

"That would make two of you," she says, smiling. Then she frowns suddenly. "We'd have to get a litter box."

I can tell she's thinking about it.

THE DIAMOND RING

Every year Grandma Rosie buys Aiden something really fine for Christmas. Last year it was a pair of Black Tack Skates, the kind Stevie Owen has — the best player in Aiden's school. The year before, she got him a telescope that he assembled, then actually could see the craters and shadows on the moon. Aiden doesn't know what she's going to get him this year but he knows it'll be something good. It's always better than what his mother gets him, although he loves her presents, too — especially the red Montreal Canadiens toque to which he is deeply attached. He wears it all the time so he won't lose it.

Aiden's mother, Julie, took him to one of the big box malls to do his Christmas shopping. It's the first time he's ever done this and she has left him to his own devices while she tries on shoes. Aiden's shoes are fine for now, although he'll likely outgrow them within a couple of months. However, his socks have holes in them, as do his pockets. She wonders how it is that small boys always have holes in their pockets. It usually means the knees will go next and then she'll have to buy him pants as well. Fortunately, Aiden's grandmother, Rosie, always buys him several pairs of socks for Christmas — these on top of the really good gift she always presents him. Julie can count on her mother for that.

The trouble is, Aiden thinks, that he never gets anything for his Grandmother, well anything good. That's because he can't afford to; he doesn't have the kind of money to compete with what she gets him. Last year, he had made her a collage from pictures cut from magazines at school. It was of a dog because he knows she liked them. Her dog had died shortly after her husband — both within a year. Aiden thought Grandpa Charles was way too grouchy, but blamed it on his illness. His Grandma Rosie is never grouchy. Neither was Patch, who despite being slow and grey, would invariably thump the floor with his tail when he saw him — except for the time he bit Aiden on the hand just hard enough to remind the boy he shouldn't tease. He wishes he could get her a dog now even though she says nothing will ever replace Patch. At any rate, he knows the cost of dogs. He's been through it with his mom: "There's no such thing as free dogs," she says.

However, Aiden also knows his Grandma Rosie likes jewellery. Gold and silver often dangle from her neck and wrists. The diamonds in them blink like snow on a moonlit night. So this year he knows what he's going to do: he's going to get her a ring. He knows exactly which one because he saw it in a flyer that was stuffed in the mailbox. "Genuine Zirconia Diamond," the ad said. "On Sale for just $23.95!"

Aiden doesn't have $23.95 to buy the ring, so he's going to steal it. He thinks it will be easy because rings are small and can fit easily into the palm of his hand. He can't wait to see his grandma's face when she opens his gift — a genuine diamond ring.

Rosaline worries that she is spoiling him, but Aiden is her only grandson and it's hard not to buy him nice things. He was so responsive to the optics of a telescope, she is buying him a camera, a digital one so he doesn't bother Julia for the film, and even though she would never figure out how to run it herself, she is sure he will. Rosaline will tell anyone who will listen that he's such a clever boy. But there is a dose of practicality in her too: the skates she bought him last year still fit him because she had bought them a wee bit large for him to grow into. Yet more than anything, Aiden always seemed genuinely appreciative of her gifts, and this was his gift in return.

Rosaline is just leaving the cash register at the photography department where she has purchased the digital camera, and is tucking the box into her bag, when she happens to look up: and there he is, parked still as a statue in front of the jewellery counter. She knows instantly it is her Aiden for he is the only boy she knows who wears a red Montreal Canadiens toque pulled down tight over his ears, indoors and out.

She has no idea what he is doing there but it seems to Rosaline as though he is waiting for something and thinking really hard. She didn't know her grandson could be so still. He actually stands out for all the bustle around him, that and his red toque showing just above the counter.

She wonders where her daughter is and thinks it's just like Julie to leave him wander alone like that; she is certainly nowhere to be seen. Julia and Aiden are all she has left now that Charles is gone. Yet she and Julia do not get along. They agree on nothing. It was Charles' job to get along with her. It was her job to get along with Aiden.

Rosaline is torn between going over and giving Aiden a big Christmas hug and just standing there watching him. Watching him while he doesn't know he is being watched. You see people as they really are when they don't know anyone's looking, that's what Rosaline believes, and it's a part of her faith too that the Good Lord sees all whether you know He's looking or not. There's no pulling the wool over His eyes.

She decides that the Christmas hug is the wiser option in this instance and just as she steps in Aiden's direction, she sees his small white hand reach up to the counter top and pluck something, and in one swift motion place his hand in his pocket. Then slowly, he walks away, his red toque bobbing down the aisle.

Rosaline is filled with a dreadful trembling. She leaves the store as quickly as aged legs will carry her.

Outside, she glances up to see herself reflected in the store window. Rosaline is hunched, carrying her bag tucked up under her chin like an old woman carries her dog. I am an old woman, she thinks. She straightens, walks upright, and takes long full strides as though Patch were pulling her along on a leash. She will not be an old woman. But Rosaline slips in the parking lot and nearly falls. Then she cannot find her car. She wanders up and down the rows, hunched again and near tears, feeling like a fool.

A young man pushing carts back into the store, stops to ask what is wrong. Nothing, she thinks, I'm just an old fool, but collects herself and describes the car. He helps find it. On the back seat lies a pair of her dead husband's work gloves; beside it, her dead dog's leash. She'd not noticed them before. She thanks the young man then climbs inside the car and throws the bag on the cold seat beside her.

On the way home, Rosaline stops at the SPCA. She will either donate the leash or fill it with a new dog. She recognizes the attendant, a young woman with blonde hair who offers Rosaline a brilliant smile. The attendant had been there when Rosaline lost Patch and had been a comfort then. She had suggested that a time might come when Rosaline would want to replace the pet that was always at her heel, and seeing her here assumes that now is the time.

She ushers Rosaline into a room filled with cages. The cages are filled with dogs. Although some dogs bark, most stand staring with their sad, resigned eyes as though they know their fate. Rosaline erupts into tears.

The attendant at the shelter has seen people break into sobs before and knows that now is not the time for Rosaline to get another dog. She holds the old lady gently, the way she had held

Patch when she assisted putting him down. But Rosaline says something inexplicable to her: she says, "I bought my grandson such nice gifts and he is a thief." She gives the attendant the leash she is holding, then goes out to the car and comes back with a pair of men's work gloves and a box. In the box is a camera. Rosaline says that perhaps she can use it to help advertise for homes for the dogs.

Aiden's mother is happy to see him back in the shoe department. She is having a difficult time finding a pair to buy: they don't have her size in the ones she likes. She is sitting amid boxes and a frustrated clerk.

"Where were you?" she asks Aiden.

"Nowhere," he says.

"Are you hot?" she asks.

"No," says Aiden.

"You look flushed," she says.

Aiden is confused for a moment. He knows you can flush a toilet, but doesn't know how it applies to him. He notices the shoes his mother is trying on; they have red laces.

"I like those ones," he says.

"Pack them," she says to the clerk.

In minutes they are through the checkout. The ring is hot in Aiden's hand. He holds tight because of the rip in his pocket.

"What's the matter?" Julie asks.

"Nothing," says Aiden. But something is the matter. The ring is burning a hole in his hand.

"Can we get Grandma a dog?" Aiden asks his mother.

"Don't be silly. Where would we get a dog?" says Julie.

This stops Aiden. He doesn't know where you get dogs but knows they must come from somewhere. "Where did Grandma get Patch?" he asks.

Julie frowns and doesn't answer. She knows that Patch came from the SPCA, but to get her mother one without her permission would not be a good idea. I should get her one anyway, she thinks.

As they push through the doors into the darkening winter afternoon, Aiden sees the look on his mother's face; it is as though she is counting things. He suddenly realizes she would ask where he got the money to buy the ring. He opens the palm of his hand and feels the cold trickle of the ring bouncing down off the inside of his pants against his leg. He knows it lies somewhere near the entranceway but does not pick it up.

Ron Mackenzie doesn't get into town that often and for good reason — he hates it. He hates the traffic, he hates the crowds, the smell of both. If it was a crop, it'd be plenteous but rotten. But it is Christmas, and Ron knows you have to go to town at Christmas.

It is Ron's observation that if you have to buy gifts for everyone, you can't do that at the Menard Co-op — not without everyone knowing what you bought and who you bought it for. It wouldn't be twenty minutes before Menard and half the surrounding area knew too. Not that there's anything wrong with people knowing what you got your wife for Christmas, unless it's Margaret Hildebrandt who tells them. It is Ron's opinion that the woman has a mouth like a megaphone.

So as much as he hates it, he knows that for certain that he has to go into town to do some anonymous Christmas shopping for Dolores, James and Jennifer.

Dolores is Ron's wife of thirty-four years; James and Jennifer, their children. It's only because they don't have grandchildren like other people their age that they call James and Jennifer their "children," for they are fully grown and live far from Menard. If it was just for his children alone, Ron wouldn't go to town to shop because he couldn't care less what Margaret Hildebrandt said about whatever he got for them. It is his bitter belief that they had made their choices, and those choices did not include him or Dolores; that they live where they want, and so be it. He has tried, but nothing he could buy would be good enough for them no matter where he bought it.

The only reason he goes to town at Christmas is for Dolores. Dolores is so pretty. He doesn't know how to tell her, but he loves to see those blue-green eyes light up, and that smile, with those lips he would walk through fire to kiss. A lot of people might think he's a sentimental fool, but he wants to get her something nice, something beyond the practical, beyond the regular domestic fare. He wants to get her something special.

He never knows what it is until he sees it. Then he knows instantly. He doesn't care what it costs, he gets it, has it boxed up, and presents it to her on Christmas morning. Just to see those eyes and kiss those lips.

Ron told Dolores he had a confession to make. He said it never cost him a cent, that he found it just outside the store and he knew she'd like it. It's not the cost, Dolores said, it's the thought that counts. When she opened the little box with the ring inside, she kissed him.

"He is such a sweet man," she tells Margaret Hildebrandt, " — provided you don't cross him, or talk to him before his second cup of coffee."

Dolores Mackenzie knows it was not an expensive ring. She also knows that Ron couldn't distinguish between a 17-carat diamond and broken coke bottle. If it was a piece of farm machinery or a handful of wheat, he would quickly inform you if it was any good or not.

But Dolores did wonder about the origin of the ring, and how it may have come to be lost. Ron could have bought better rings at the Menard Co-op where the manager's wife had attached a small hair salon and jewellery store — not that he would ever go in there. In Dolores's words, Ron cannot abide Margaret Hildebrandt, and when Ron takes a dislike to someone, there's no going back. She thinks he was sweet on her once, that's her theory — but it would have been a long time ago. He's a devoted, loving husband and Dolores treasures him more than anything he could ever buy.

So Dolores cannot say how upset she is at losing the ring. She is equally upset by the way she lost it. She could never tell Ron about it either, and he'll never know because Dolores has sworn Margaret to secrecy — besides, she knows it's a safe bet he'll never talk to her anyway.

The Mackenzies live just north of Menard, about two miles, then a mile east on the old school grid. There's only one other farm there and that belongs to the Hildebrandts, Bud and Margaret. The Hildebrandts are their nearest neighbours, but not their closest. Today, Dolores needs flour. She thought she had lots, but the children are coming home for Easter and she likes to have extra baking around just in case. En route to the Menard Co-op, she notices a pair of ravens catching the currents that rise above the bluff. She pauses to watch their wilful play — the sun bouncing off their back and wings as they twist and slide up, then down. However, she is hardly past the Hildebrandt's lane, when she sees Margaret, on the side of the road, rooting through her car trunk like an old red hen at the feed bin. Dolores stops.

"What you doing, Margaret?" she asks.

"I got a damn flat tire," answers Margaret.

"Where's Bud?" asks Dolores.

"He's in the bush," Margaret says.

Dolores understands immediately that it is the beginning of bear season, and that Bud is a big hunter who likes to get out before the Americans hit. She considers Margaret for a moment, a large woman, likely with diabetes and probably high blood pressure too. Lugging that wheel out of the trunk and changing the tire all by herself might be dangerous to her health.

"I'll give you a hand," she says.

There is plenty of mud on the road. Getting the jack beneath the car frame makes for muddy red knuckles and soaked knees. The lug nuts are welded on with ten years of rust, and Dolores jumps on the tire iron to loosen them. It takes all of her weight and series of mild oaths.

They get the job done in about a half an hour. Margaret had assisted as best she could, but really, it was Dolores who did most of the work. Nevertheless, they are both covered nearly head to toe in mud and are a spectacle. Dolores hears the ravens laugh.

"I can't go in to work like this," says Margaret, as much to herself as to Dolores. Then, "Come on back up and I'll call in late. We need a scrubbing."

Dolores concedes that there is no point in her traipsing the half-mile back home to dirty up her bathroom, and she follows Margaret down lane.

It isn't till she is drying her hands that Dolores notices the ring is gone. An instant panic sets in. It's not the value of it, it's the thought behind it.

They scrounge the area where they had changed the tire, but it is nowhere to be found. It is simply gone.

So the ring Dolores now wears is not the one Ron had given her; the ring she wears comes from the Menard Co-op. Margaret said they were on sale.

Raven sees the world in another dimension. To him, Dolores and Margaret are creatures with flat faces. They walk on their hind legs only — like bear when he is angry — and are not to be trusted. He has tried to comprehend what cars are and has determined that they are huge, growling eggs capable of eating the flat faces and disgorging them at will. It also seems to him that the shiny eggs have trails, same as deer, but much larger, and they hunt along these paths. The eggs are not effective hunters but kill enough deer and other animals along their paths to make scavenging worthwhile. For some inexplicable reason, the eggs do not seem interested in eating what they kill. So Raven eats with other ravens, until the sharp-faces come — fox and coyote. Then Raven stands aside.

This day, two growling eggs have stopped upon their path. Two flat-faces have climbed out of their shiny shells. The flat-faces huddle near the ground. Perhaps they look for kill. There is none. Raven turns beneath the sun. The flat-faces climb back into their shells. The eggs roar away.

Raven alights where they have been and looks for food the flat faces sometimes leave. He finds none. Instead, he finds a hard, shiny stone attached to the shape of a new moon. He takes it in his beak as he flies across the sky. Raven plants the shiny moon in his nest.

He calls for his mate.

Wag is Aiden's dog, a large, friendly taffy-coloured mutt so named because of the way her tail seemed to wag her. She has been Aiden's companion since she was a pup, twelve years ago. Now he shares an apartment with her not far from where his grandmother once lived.

Wag and Aiden's usual route is out along the river bank where they stroll in the evening after work — Aiden's work — Wag is retired. Aiden is a certified optician and there's nothing better than fresh air after eight hours being trapped inside with the filtered, artificial atmosphere of his workplace.

Wag's not sure what she and Aiden are doing here this cool fall day kicking through the leaves between the gravestones. "It's too cold," she's saying. "My arthritis is acting up. And, this isn't our usual route." Wag's getting up there in dog years and not moving quite as well as she once did. But Aiden thought she should come along to visit his grandmother Rosaline's grave. Wag was her dog only a few short months before she died suddenly and unexpectedly — the year she had given him only socks for Christmas.

There's something Aiden needs to do that takes him here, away from their usual route, where they walked a day earlier, following a vicious fall storm. Power lines were knocked down by falling trees; branches and shingles were strewn everywhere. It had been a miracle no one was hurt in the violence of the wind. A number of fallen trees had blocked the route along their path.

Suddenly, Wag loped on ahead of Aiden, and went sniffing into the crown of an elm that lay sprawled before them. Her big old tail swept from side to side. She'd found something.

Aiden went to investigate.

There, lying among the tangle of brush was a raven's nest. It had broken apart but in it lay a glittering pile of debris: coke tabs, bits of tin foil, CDs, coins — at least a dozen golf balls — and amidst it all, a ring.

Aiden scraped his hand reaching among the twist and tangle of twigs that had once made the raven's nest. He recognized the ring instantly, then examined it more closely: He had studied that ring before. He was suddenly nine years old again, peering above the counter in the jewellery department. It had lost its store-counter sheen. A fine grime lay in the seams of the setting, but the zircon still winked in the sun. He clutched it, cool and solid in his hand.

The ring is why Wag and Aiden are at the cemetery.

With his apartment key, Aiden breaks through a crust of ground and scrapes a hollow beside his grandmother Rosaline's headstone. In it he places the ring.

"Merry Christmas, Grandma," he says.

Wag grumbles at an old couple who pass nearby.

A raven flies overhead.

FEEDING PIRANHA

Joseph Pollen has been nominated twice for a Governor General's Award in poetry but never won. He has fourteen books to his credit. My personal favourite is *Feeding Piranha*, an epic poem full of the starkest, purest verse ever placed upon a page. I have no idea what most of it means, but its violent images cling to you like fish-stink. I'm on a pilgrimage to meet him and acquire a letter of reference that he has agreed to write on my behalf. This will accompany my grant application to the provincial arts board — my first one. My name is Lyle Mackenzie and I'm a poet. I'm also a little nervous.

I expect a small, tidy man — perhaps with glasses, those wire-rimmed type that perch on your nose. He responded briefly to my letter indicating that I should come on up any time during the day, during the week. The address is in a poorer part of town. Tall caraganas hide the yard and you almost have to enter through the gate sideways to avoid the hanging foliage. The house is small and tattered — a shack really. I knock on the door. Blistered paint falls off.

"It's open!" a voice hollers from within.

I enter.

A bulky, barefoot man fills the room. A wiry grey goatee dangles from his chin. His face is punctuated by a red, twisted nose. "Welcome!" he says. "This is my office!" He flourishes his arm as though it's the executive suite at the Ritz where in reality four faded green walls hang from a dark, pustular and fly-speckled ceiling. The room is bare of any adornment except for a drugstore calendar tacked next to the doorway. It isn't on the right month. He'd stopped flipping the pages in February.

The August heat saps the energy from the flies beating against the curtainless window trying to escape into the yard beyond, filled with broken weeds that tangle for attention all yellow and gray.

I must be staring.

"It's okay, you can't see it in winter," he says, popping a can of beer, smoke rising from a yellow cigarette. He sprawls across the only chair in the room — a colossal broken-down maroon armchair, surrounded by books, ashtrays, papers and empty cans of Pilsner beer.

He wears a plaid flannel lumberjack shirt. The shirt pocket stirs. A small white mouse emerges. Mr. Pollen hangs the mouse by the tail.

"Curious are you?" he says to the mouse. "Walter, this is Lyle. Lyle — Walter."

I nod. I've never been introduced to a mouse before. He drops it back into his pocket and buttons it shut.

He watches me search the room. There is nowhere else to sit. Or nowhere obvious.

He puts the can to his yellow teeth. "Over there," he says through the can, and points a bent finger at a stack of books. "You can sit there, next to my desk."

His desk is the stove. A door, possibly the one to his basement, which doesn't seem to have one, lays across the burners. On it sits an ancient computer that bangs and whirrs even though it is not in use. Its monitor is monochrome. The cursor flashes and winks its evil amber eye.

"The trouble with technology is it's never satisfied. It always wants more — and wants more faster." He leans forward and examines his toenails.

"You ever seen nails like these? They never stop growing," he says. "They are perfect technology. More, always more. Fast too. You got to keep on top of them." He sets the beer can on the chair's arm, and hugging his knee to his chest, pulls his foot closer to his face. For a brief moment, I think he's going to put it in his mouth. "I don't have clippers," he says, letting his foot go. It flops back onto the floor.

"Would you like a drink?" he asks, splashing some of his beer from the can.

"I don't drink."

"You don't drink!" He roars.

"In the morning," I say.

"Well it's noon somewhere, and I'm the bartender." He clambers out of the chair.

"No, really . . . " I falter.

"Ah, holding out for the good stuff," he says slapping his bare feet across the room. He flings open the door to a solitary cupboard and pulls down a green bottle.

"So do you smoke?"

"Er, no."

"Gamble? Womanize? You must do something."

"Womanize I guess."

"Well thank God for that. And now you'll drink. This . . . ," he holds up the bottle, " . . . is the finest shine this side of the moon. You don't even have to swallow, just place it on your tongue and resist passing out." He chuckles and grabs a cup from a cluttered pile of crockery that rise from the porcelain sink and shakes it.

"I'd rinse it, but if I turn the tap on the toilet will back up. Don't ask."

He pours a clear liquid from the green bottle into the cup.

"Don't worry. Anything living in it a few seconds ago is now dead. Cheers!" he says passing me the cup and smacking it with the bottle. He takes a swig. "Drink!" he commands.

I drink.

Suddenly, the air in the room vanishes. Or has become molten lava. I can't tell which.

"That'll put some hair on your knuckles." He takes another swig.

Tears fill my eyes. My skull implodes. I teeter on the stack of books that is my chair. I had barely wet my tongue. Which I can only feel with my teeth. Which have sprouted nerve endings.

I study my knuckles. Hair grows.

"The product, they say, of fine copper and rotting grain," he says.

I nod. So that's what I had inhaled.

"You'd think they'd get caught, you know, but they never do."

I have no idea what he's talking about. It must show.

"The folks who make this." He holds up the bottle. "They've been doing it for decades, for as long as anyone can remember, and they've never been caught. Some day they will be and we'll all be sad." He takes another swig and wipes the back of his arm with his mouth. "But I guess everything has to end sometime, eh? What do you say there, sport? Smoke? Ah, that's right, I asked you that already. You don't. You womanize."

"I don't know if womanize is the right word."

"No? Finding the right word is what it's all about, isn't it. What's the right word?"

"I don't know. I have a girlfriend."

"Oh! A girl friend. A girlfriend . . . " He looks out the window at the sunburnt weeds as though he might see her there picking daisies. "Yes, girlfriends are good." Then he turns to me. "So you don't actually womanize then."

"No, not actually, no."

"You're only batting two-fifty there Lyle. And you better drink up or you won't even be batting that."

I look at the liquid in the bottom of my cup. How did this become my batting average? I used to play baseball. In baseball, two-fifty is a pretty good average. Oh, I get it. I don't smoke, gamble or womanize. I drink. One out of four.

"Okay, okay, I'll get you some mix." He gathers himself to rise from his chair, flops his feet across the floor and in one deft move, springs open the handleless fridge with a butter knife. "I hate diluting it but I guess you had a taste of it straight. That's how it should be drunk." He unscrews a two-litre plastic bottle of ginger ale as he walks towards me. It fizzes briefly. He fills my cup to the brim.

"Remind me again why you're here?"

"The letter," I begin.

"Oh yes, to write you a letter." He flops back into the armchair. "Why should I write you a letter? Tell me about yourself."

I open my mouth to speak but nothing comes out. I don't know where to begin. Family? School? My writing? Do I tell him I might have finished first in the poetry slam where the prize was to actually get published by a real, genuine literary magazine, *Ergot*, that publishes people like him, Margaret Atwood and other famous dead poets who might yet be alive? Did he want to know about this? If there hadn't been penalty points for running overtime I would have won?

Or would that be boasting?

"Like what do you want to know?"

"Oh never mind, it doesn't matter. Did it matter that I wanted to be a writer? Not for an instant — either you are or you aren't. Sometimes it takes a lifetime to find out. In the end, it doesn't matter if you are or you aren't. Nobody knows the difference — except other writers." He laughs in long drawn-out caws at what he thinks is a huge joke, then settles into a grand fit of coughing and turns red while his eyes bulge out. I think I may be watching him die. I'm wondering if he has a phone. Or if he does — where he hides it.

But he recovers, wipes his mouth again and continues. His shirt pocket stirs. Walter wants out.

"Why would anybody want to be a writer? For all this?" He throws his hands up to include the room. "Be careful what you ask for. You might become one. Writing is something you do. Being a writer is something you are. It pulls you onto the page like ink — YOU!" He points at me with a gnarled yellow finger. "Being a writer plucks your eyeballs from their sockets and sets them down in front of you to gaze into your own soul. And if you don't like what you see there, guess what? Nobody gives a rat's ass. Not for a second."

"I do," I say.

"What the hell do you know? Come here," he says. "I want to show you something." He crosses the room to a closed door. He opens it then turns to me. "Are you coming or not?"

I hadn't realized he wanted me to follow. As I rise from my perch, he enters the room.

It's his bedroom. It's almost as large as his "office" and it's hot enough to melt lead. It is filled with a large, unmade bed next to a dresser. On the dresser is a reading lamp and stacks of books. The lamp casts a feeble yellow light against a dark green wall that frames a green and yellow flag of Saskatchewan. It's hung by the top corners and sags in the middle. On the other side of the bed, a large, lit fish tank sits bubbling on a metal rack; beside it stands a wardrobe, next to a window — venetian blinds shut tight. Below the window is small wooden table and chair heaped with papers. A copy of the application I sent him seems to leap from the clutter.

He sits on the edge of the bed holding a small, framed picture. He studies it. Then turns it towards me. A blonde girl smiles, squinting into the sun.

"Pretty isn't she."

"Yes, very."

"My sister, Lillian" he says. "Don't get any ideas — it was taken twenty years ago. She's the only one in the family who still talks to me. She doesn't live here so it doesn't happen much."

A pause happens here. I can't tell if he's running out of steam, or gathering it.

"Where does she live?"

"China. The rest of them, four brothers and a sister, live right here. They didn't even tell me when mom died. So I missed her funeral. Lillian did too — but then that's because she's in China, not because she wrote the 'Ode to Bunny'."

"I read that. It was removed from our school curriculum."

"Yes, well, Bunny is my brother's wife. You shouldn't mention your brother's wife's yellow teeth in a poem. You should avoid discussing her pink pudendum. More importantly, you shouldn't refer to them from your brother's point of view. And if you do, you shouldn't get it published."

"It shouldn't win the Ben Tiller Award either."

"No, that doesn't help." Suddenly he turns. "Look at that flag. You see that flag? Look carefully at the tiger lily. What do you see on the tiger lily?"

I squint, searching the flag's tiger lily. I look high and low. There is dust on its hanging folds. "Dust?"

"No, not dust! Pollen! My family's name is sewn into the very fabric of the Saskatchewan flag! And half of them thought that 'Ode' was a travesty, an invasion of privacy, a betrayal of the good name of Pollen and a desecration of the flag of Saskatchewan. The other half defended me till the court case came.

"Even though the judge threw it out, they all decided it was easier to avoid me than each other and that's how come they don't talk to me anymore. I lost my entire family because of one poem. Except Lillian. Who missed it all.

"Still, it was worth it. I got a voice out of it. It all boils down to voice. If you don't have a voice, you don't have anything. I have my brother's voice, the voice of a speckled man in a brown suit with wire-rimmed glasses. People are always shocked to meet me. I'm glad they're shocked. It proves that I made something that they imagined. And I made them imagine it. That's the power of being a writer. And you'll sell your family to get it. Are you ready for that?" Flecks of foam hang from the corner of his mouth. His goatee shivers.

"I think so."

"You think so? That's it — you think so?"

"I know so."

"And how do you know that?"

"How?"

"How."

Of course, I don't know anything. I'm just giving him the answers I think he wants to hear, the ones he seems to be prompting me for.

"I don't know if I'm ready for anything but I believe I have to start somewhere."

Joseph Pollen's eyes go huge for a moment. His eyeballs tip over the edge of their sockets. "Jesus Murphy," he mutters, "Jesus Murphy." Then he sprints from the room leaving me standing there beside his bed. There is a splash in the aquarium. One lonely fish swims about. I wonder if he's trying to escape.

"This calls for another drink!" Joe says dashing back through the door, dousing my cup with more liquids. "That was the most honest answer I have ever received. You just might be doomed to be a poet! Cheers!" He drinks straight from the bottle. I do what I can without choking.

"Let me look at those sample poems you sent . . . " He grabs at the pile on the table. He reads.

> Yesterday stands or walks
> as I stand or walk
> and if I turn too suddenly
> I can see how
> all those children
> had their mothers' eyes.

That's not bad. Good beginning. Good ending. But you know what there, Lyle?"

"What?"

"It's got no middle."

"It's too short?"

"It doesn't go far enough. It's not developed. In thirty or forty years you'll be able to write a hell of a middle. You just need a bit of time."

"Forty years?"

"If it doesn't eat you up first. Time's a brutal beast. Surviving is half the battle. If you make it to thirty, and are still writing, you'll likely die with a pen in your hand — or staring at the blank screen. It never gets any easier, you know — you get better at it, but it never gets any easier. What do you know about fish?"

"Fish? I don't know. They have fins."

"Besides that."

"They swim?"

"What else."

I am wondering if there is a punch line to this. "They have bones that get stuck in your throat; they stink; they, they like water . . . " I'm being a smart-ass; the shine has gone to my head.

"Yes, but what do they do for a living?" he interrupts.

"For a living? I have no idea."

"They eat! They don't play chess or shave or change their shorts or learn how to type or drive a car — they eat. That's it."

I don't know where he's going with this. I'm still a bit shook-up with waiting till I'm fifty to finish my poem. How does he explain Byron, Shelley, Keats and the rest of those guys who didn't make forty — Dylan Thomas?

"What does this have to do with poetry?"

"Well you see, we poets are just like fish, except we don't eat for a living, we write poems. If we don't write poems, we die."

"We'll die if we don't eat too."

"That's true, but a fish won't die if he doesn't write a poem. So the question is, what are you, a fish or a poet?"

I suppose my mouth is hanging open gulping at air outside the tank. I see where he's going now.

"What do you suppose happened to those brilliant boys — the Byrons and Shelleys who were lucky to make thirty?"

"Are you saying . . . ?"

"That's what I'm saying."

"Dylan Thomas?"

"Dylan Thomas too. They stopped writing." He mimes slicing his throat. "Suicide."

I take a good long drink of my alcohol co-mingled ginger ale. I notice I am sweating.

"Hot," I say.

"You want to know why?"

I'm afraid to ask.

"He needs it that way," he says pointing at the fish. "You probably noticed he swims alone. It's not that he's unsociable really — he gets along well with his own kind — but he eats any living thing I put in there."

Its dead, flat eyes are too big for its body and its steely mouth has a serious overbite. "Piranha?"

"They feast communally but have terrible table manners, ripping the flesh off God's living creatures to the bone — a million tiny, vicious bites. They don't even leave the gristle."

"Feeding Piranha."

"You got it. The act of feeding piranha is sometimes treacherous. Feeding piranha themselves are definitely hazardous."

Joseph Pollen unbuttons the pocket on his shirt, pulls the small white rodent into the light and dangles it by the tail.

"So," he caws, dropping Walter into the tank. "Which are you, kid?"

ELK DOG

My Grandfather Lee sits in his wheelchair looking a lot like Chief Dan George. In fact, the older he gets, the more he looks like the movie star: the same long braids of silver hair; the wise, dark, twinkling eyes; the soft, down-turned lips and overall, the same peanutty hued flesh full of valleys and creeks.

"Oh yes," he says. "Oh, yes."

These are the only words Grandfather Lee has.

If you ask, "How are you today?" he can't answer. If you add, "Good?" and he says, "Oh, yes!" then you know. If he doesn't answer or looks away, the answer is "no." This is how he communicates.

He's had a stroke.

He was a vet — not the soldier kind — he practiced veterinarian medicine. His specialty was large animals. But that only partially explains the horses.

Grandfather Lee collected horses. He collected them like others collect antique cars or baseball cards. He knew a great deal about them, not only their physiology, but their history, including when and where and why they were bred. He knew, for instance, that the Akhal-Teke was originally bred in Asia as a war horse, and that Appaloosas were first known as "Palouse

Horses" because they were selected, bred and ridden by the Nez Percé, from that area of northwestern states. He knew that the Nez Percé have legendary abilities with horses and today breed Akhal-Tekes with Apaloosas. He knew that the Piegans were at first afraid of horses, until they learned to put packs on them like they did their dogs. They called the animal *ponokah-mita* or elk dog. He thought this knowledge was a way of informing himself of his heritage of which he knew nothing. He was adopted, but his ancestry shows on his face.

There is no proof of his ancestry, only the looks. They have skipped a generation and show on me. Just on me, not my brother.

"Chink eyes!"

"Indian!"

"Wagon Burner!"

"Half-breed!"

I've been called them all — including "apple," red outside, white in. You can see it mostly in my eyes and maybe the cheekbones. I tan really easy in summer and my toasty hue seems to hang on long after the first snow falls. I don't properly pale up till February. My brother Harley, on the other hand, is the colour of milk. I don't care about getting called the names. I mention it to Harley. He takes care of things. There's more than one kid with damaged cartilage in his nose who finds it hard to breathe. They now address me by my proper name, Jay.

I love Harley. I would do anything for him. I owe him.

Five years ago, the summer was hot, and although the sun baked the days, its heat seldom lingered past dusk. Our cold damp sleeping bags waited alone in cold damp tents. Around the campfire, we fixed our gazes into the radiant orange heat — too tired and too lazy to move. The flames danced inside the smoke and snapped their fingers against the night sky.

"What causes that sound?" I asked.

"What sound?" asked Harley.

"The fire snapping," I said.

Although the question was thrown out above the rising glow, only one person would answer. And after a brief pause, Grandfather Lee considered his words and spoke.

"That, they tell me, is the sound of gases exploding," he said.

Grandfather Lee always gave the perfect answer — if he knew it. And if he didn't, he'd tell you that too. "That is a conundrum, to both me and my horse," he'd say. No one knew to which of his horses he was referring. He had several, but he never rode them. No one rode them. They were retired, like Grandfather Lee.

In the three years since Aunt Ellen died, Grandfather Lee's singular discernable activity away from his acreage was a pilgrimage with me and Harley to someplace quiet and serene — a lake, say, or an escarpment behind a river — filled with creatures that buzzed or chirped or cawed and otherwise remained hidden in the undergrowth. A canoe was involved in these trips. It was as orange as fire. We paddled and portaged it to these remote sites. Harley and Grandfather Lee would carry the canoe. I would scramble along behind carrying whatever I could for I was younger and, of course, smaller. This would be the first year that I would be allowed a chance to paddle. But I also wondered why we'd never gone riding on Grandfather's horses.

"Why don't we go on a trail ride with your horses?" I asked.

"Horses are really bad at paddling," said Grandfather Lee. "Besides, they're retired."

"You're retired," I said..

"Yes, but I'm a really good paddler."

Although the logic was baffling, the fact was true that Grandfather Lee was a terrific paddler. It was a good thing too because despite being almost full-grown at seventeen, Harley's draws, pivots, sideslips and braces were as bad as Grandfather Lee's were good. The only reason he paddled at all was because he wouldn't let me do it. Too embarrassing.

While on the water, I sat amid the provisions in the centre of the boat alternately dozing and staring into the blue-green stone-studded bottom. Every now and then something would prod me to break my reverie with a question — like seeing a fish dart by.

"How do fish breathe?" I asked once.

"Through their nose," Harley responded.

"They don't have noses," I said.

"Actually, they do," Grandfather Lee finally interjected, "they just don't use them for breathing — just for smelling. Fish have gills that comb the oxygen right out of the water and on into their hearts. They don't need lungs."

I envisioned a sort of special fishy comb with really fine teeth to rake the water for O_2 molecules like Mom raked the lawn for leaves.

He went on to explain the whole incomprehensible series of events involving oxygen diffusing, hemoglobin, and iron, then ended, "but if I was a fish, I'd wonder how humans combed the oxygen molecules out of the air so they could breathe."

"What do you mean?" A whole new screen flashed in front of my mind's eye, but the images were incomplete, mis-formed. People didn't breathe through combs on the sides of their necks like fish. People had noses instead.

"Well air is mostly nitrogen — eighty percent they tell me, but our bodies just use the oxygen . . . " he said.

"Ho-lee!" I would say, wonder at it all, then recommit to my reverie somewhat wiser and much more happy.

But this night, with the camp set halfway through a portage and around the snapping flames, Grandfather Lee was the one to ask a question. He nodded a bit as though agreeing with something he'd thought of, then his eyes widened into a great surprised look. "How long the mirthip?" he asked.

"What?"

"Huh?" said Harley.

"Reluf a menthith-ththth . . . "

Grandfather Lee pitched onto his side. His right side, pinning his arm beneath him. He reached out with his left, clawing at the air. He still wore the same surprised look on his face. He moved his mouth like a fish out of water.

We both jumped up, "Grandpa!" Harley immediately tried to prop him back onto his perch, but realized he'd have to stay there holding him to remain upright.

"Get his sleeping bag!" Harley yelled.

I scrambled to my grandfather's tent, grabbed the bag and returned. I tried draping it over Grandfather's shoulders but Harley was in the way.

"Just lay it on the ground!" said Harley.

"I am!" I hadn't been but did as my brother suggested.

Harley slowly eased Grandfather to the ground as I attempted to arrange the bag around him.

"It's okay, Grandpa. It's going to be all right." The words came out of my mouth automatically.

"Yeah," said Harley. "Everything's going to okay."

We looked at one another and knew that everything was not going to be all right or okay, that something terrible had happened to Grandfather Lee and that we had to get him somewhere for treatment. We also knew that this would not be an easy task. That this might be an impossible task. We did not speak these thoughts, but we knew them.

"We need a plan," said Harley.

"We need a helicopter." One had passed over the day before. "Maybe we can harness these mosquitoes," I added, trying to make a joke.

"Get lots of wood. We'll stay out by the fire," said Harley.

A low rumble rolled in from the night sky.

"Geez, is it going to rain?" Harley asked aloud. He didn't expect an answer. It was more an observation than a question.

"It feels like it, doesn't it," I agreed.

"Let's get the canoe. We can put it over him just in case," said Harley. This would be easier than trying to haul our stricken grandfather into his tent, and it would probably be as dry.

In less than twenty minutes, the rain came. It fell in cataracts, smothering the fire and, although our heads remained dry huddled inside the overturned canoe, the water seeped under us and wicked up our clothes. We tried stuffing our sleeping bags beneath Grandfather to keep him drier but our efforts were futile, and very soon meaningless.

A huge crack of thunder shook the air around us and the blue light cut like a silver axe through the dark. The acrid smell of ozone stung our nostrils from the nearby strike.

With his good hand, Grandfather Lee reached from under the canoe and dragged the small camp shovel to his side. Then, with great difficulty, tried to raise it, offering it to Harley.

"Dig? You want me do dig?" said Harley.

"Oh, yes!" said his grandfather.

"Here, now?"

"Yes, yes!" he said.

"What do we want to dig in the rain for?" Harley asked.

"Maybe to get away from the fire," I was looking into the forest..

"What fire?"

"That fire," I said pointing to the glow that grew in the wet black.

We dug. First Harley dug, then when he tired, I took the shovel. We shovelled amid the muck and rain. We shovelled as though our lives depended on it. Our lives did depend on it. When the hole was deep enough, we hauled Grandfather into it, covered ourselves with branches and the over-turned canoe then hunkered beneath it all and waited for the fire to come.

"How do you know this is going to work?" I asked.

"I saw it in a movie," Harley said.

"I never saw that movie." Harley often went to movies without me. "Did you see it Grandpa?"

"Oh, yes," he said.

"It's the safest place to be. Fires burn up, not down," said Harley.

"You sound like Grandpa," I said.

"We saw the same movie," said Harley.

As the fire approached, we could hear it roaring louder and louder, and in the spaces between our covering branches, we saw the flames exploding from the trees above, dancing from one to the next. But Harley was right. We were untouched. Our foxhole remained cool and damp — wet. We stayed there till dawn.

Harley was the first out to survey the campsite and surrounding countryside. The rain had long since stopped — and as near as we could make out, so had the fire. But we were in the middle of a burn. The bare black timber stabbed into the stark blue sky. Our tents had partially dissolved and hung blackened from the poles that still held their skeletal shapes. Smoke rose here and there from smouldering mounds. Yet, we ourselves hadn't been touched. Some ash had scorched-pocked the canoe bottom. Otherwise nothing.

Soon, a spotter plane passed overhead. We waved frantically. The plane dipped its wings from one side to the other — the pilot acknowledging that he'd seen us. Two hours later, the helicopter arrived.

Some events change things forever. The event will have an image to go with it that is burned into our psyches: the mushroom cloud; the jet flying into the skyscraper; the president's head snapping back in the open limo. These are global examples. On a personal level, we each have our own. For Harley and I, it is Grandpa falling sideways in front of the fire, the surprised look on his face. And the rest of the night spent in a hole while rain and fire raged above us.

There is no explaining the effect of those events. They leave different marks on each of us.

Elk Dog

In the five years since grandpa's stroke, I have become an expert in horses. I have cared for his herd and have learned a lot. I'm in first year pre-vet med and although I have a long way to go, I know I'll eventually follow in his footsteps. I am following in his footsteps. And like him, my looks betray me. They are not part of who I am. I have little interest in my heritage. I don't want to go there.

Harley, on the other hand, has climbed into another hole. The fire still burns above him. Perhaps in him. He has gone looking for his roots, but he has found the weakest branches — the gangs, the street life, the drugs. He has come to me. He wears his colours. He looks shrunken and hollow. His eyes have that film common to druggies. He's just recently had a fix.

"What are you on?" I ask.

"*Ponokah-mita*," he says laughing. "I'm riding high."

He is making a Piegan joke. "Elk dog" he is saying — horse. He is high on heroin.

Suddenly his gaunt grey face goes still. "I want to quit," he says. "I need to get away."

"Sure," I say. "Where would you like to go?"

"Remember the canoe, the night of the fire? The night grandpa . . . "

"Yes," I cut him off.

"Let's find the canoe."

The last time I saw the canoe was from the rising helicopter. It grew smaller as we flew away, its black-pocked bottom on the orange made it look like a slender lady bug. I remember thinking that.

"When do you want to go?"

"Tonight," says Harley.

"I have an exam tomorrow," I say.

"Tonight," says Harley.

I need to save my brother.

The next morning we are on the river. Since we were last here, I have become acquainted with handling a canoe. I am at the stern while Harley tries his best at the bow. He is weakened by his addiction and he was never a great paddler to begin with. Every few hours we need to stop while Harley makes himself another fix. He promises he will stop altogether when we find the canoe, or, if we don't find it, the place where we last saw it — the hole we dug, over which it lie.

Yet, we paddle; I go into that reverie, that place when everything is perfect: the air is clear and bright; the water glass; the bugs caught off in a breeze. I somehow incorporate the threatening roar that looms ahead into my focus on the howling white sun, but as we round a bend, the spectacle of churning, boiling water leaps before us. We plunge into it. It's like being slapped awake. Suddenly the keel beneath us collides rumbling over the rocks and sends a rake of fear up my back. There is no time to make careful decisions about alternate routes or safe, sweaty portages. The white torrents pounding and slashing the mammoth boulders lend my arms strength I never knew I had. My lungs burn and the gristle in my knees rolls hard against the canoe floor while sweat stings my eyes. I draw and pry or pivot through the interminable, ripping eddies, trying not to sideslip — or worse — end up in the water. I do all this virtually solo. Harley barely draws a goon stroke; he sits frozen in front of me. We rip sidelong against some ancient protruding Precambrian shield, and I am amazed that water doesn't gush through the tumblehome or just swamp us altogether.

We are swung wide around another bend and immediately in our path is a sweeper. The tree is so huge it almost spans the stream. There is no time to do any manoeuvring.

"Duck!" I scream.

Harley remains upright till the very last second when he folds backward as I lean forward. Our heads touch. Spruce branches rake over us; we squeeze through. Then just as suddenly, all is quiet. We're finally through into the clean, murmuring flow — the roar behind us.

I laugh.Harley turns and looks at me, like what am I laughing at?

The journey is more forlorn and rugged than my memory of it. No doubt Grandfather Lee's gentle company and self-assuredness is part of the reason it seems this way. I must also remember that I did not paddle the first time up this river: I was a passenger sitting between the thwarts along with our camping supplies.

Soon enough, just as we approach our portage landing, we hit the burn area. There is nothing green above a metre high. But up to that height, it is thick in willow, dogwood and black poplar. Otherwise a million charred spires point skyward as far as the eye can see.

We leave our canoe at the landing and begin hiking to where we camped at the middle of the portage. As portages go, it's a long one, over a kilometre but the trail is relatively easy to follow because it's so close to the shore.

"I need to rest," Harley says. He slumps onto a black fallen tree. "I'm out," he says. "I got no more. No more elk dog." He smiles weakly. He is sweating profusely. His breathing is harsh and shallow. "I don't even have smokes. You got any?"

"No." I sit beside him.

"You're so clean you squeak." I know he is trying to make a joke. I smile.

The insects find us immediately. I can stand the mosquitoes but I hate the black flies. Harley seems impervious. The black flies are crawling around his eyes.

"How can you stand those flies?" I ask.

"What flies?"

"The ones around your eyes."

"They're flies?" He swipes at his eyes with the back of his hand. "I thought I was imagining them. I thought they were the worms starting. I would pick them out. I don't want to start. You might have to tie me up."

Within twenty minutes, we come upon the campsite. Incredibly, remnants of the tents still stand as they had been left. The hole we'd dug is now filled with prickly rose and asters. The canoe though has been moved — nearer the shore. And it has somehow changed colour. This canoe is green.

"This isn't our canoe. Someone has swapped." I turn it over onto its keel. "This one's got some damage in the bow. I imagine it'll still float though. Should we take it back? Or leave it?"

Harley doesn't answer. His back is to me. He is holding his face in his hands.

"Harley?"

He turns and the blood from his eyes trickle down his sunken grey cheeks.

"I need you to do something," he says. "It's starting."

"You name it," I say.

"Tie my hands up."

"What?

"Tie my hands."

"Are you sure?"

"I'll rip my face off otherwise."

The painter still hangs from the battered canoe. I cut it off and began to bind Harley's hands in front of him.

"Behind my back," he says.

"This is stupid. I'm not going to tie your hands behind your back."

"Jay, I need to get through this. I need to do it now."

"You need professional help. This is bullshit," I say.

"You are my help. There's no helicopter going to swoop down and take us to a hospital or some kind of treatment centre. This is my treatment centre. You are my treatment centre."

I tie his hands.

"Thank you," he says. "Now I need to be alone." He is dismissing me.

"I'll leave," I say.

"You won't leave. You'll pretend to leave, but you'll hide some place and watch me."

"Well then how are you going to be alone?"

"Put the canoe in the water."

"What? No! I'm not going to do that. That's crazy."

"You don't know what crazy is. Put the canoe in the water or I'll do it myself."

"You can't!"

"Watch me." With his foot, he drags the canoe across the ground. He looks like a little kid wearing one of his father's shoes. It will take him awhile, but he's right — he is managing to drag it to the shore.

"You can't paddle," I say.

"You're right. I'm lousy at it."

"No, I mean there are no paddles." The paddles have disappeared along with our original canoe. "Harley, you can't go into those rapids like that. You'll die."

"I'll be 'up the creek without a paddle.'"

"I'm not going to let you," I grab the canoe.

"Let go," he says.

I pull. He loses his balance and stumbles. Quickly regaining himself he scrambles to his feet and begins kicking at me. I am surprised by his agility and quickness. He lands a hard blow to my wrist. I let go.

"Touch it again and I'll kick you in the head. I've done it before." I believe him. He hadn't done it to me, of course, but he has done it to someone. I stand in helpless terror watching my brother drag the canoe to the water's edge. This is ten times worse than watching Grandpa Lee have a stroke. What happened to him was an accident of fate. This is no such thing.

"I need to be alone," Harley says again. Enough of the canoe is in the water that it is in danger of being swept away by the current. He grabs onto it almost kneeling with his hands behind his back. He tries to get in. If he lets go to climb inside, the canoe will slip away. "Hold it," he says to me.

"No."

"Hold the canoe for me Jay. I need to do this."

"Do it yourself."

He leans forward and puts his face in the water. He holds it there. Involuntarily, I hold my own breath till suddenly Harley explodes upward, shaking the water from his face and hair. Much of the blood has washed away. His face is clearer. "You're right," he says. "Help me get it ashore."

As I take hold of the stern deck, he jumps into the canoe.

"Sucker," he says. "Now let go."

I hold on.

"Jay, please let go."

I tighten my grip.

Then he hisses, "Let go, Apple."

I let go.

"Thank you," he says. "I'm sorry. Take care of those horses." He sits between the thwarts facing the stern — backwards. It really doesn't matter. I watch as the current sweeps him downstream bouncing him between the rips and rocks. The water is high this time of year. How'll he make it to the lake?

I tell Grandfather Lee this story. He is the only one. The police would never understand.

"What would you do, Grandpa?" I ask. "Same as me?"

Grandpa doesn't answer. His face is turned down. His eyes are closed. I wonder if he is combing oxygen from the air.

BACKSTORIES

It has always fascinated me how the story about the story — the preamble — can be as interesting as the story itself — sometimes more so. There are two versions of this preamble: one has to do with how the artist came to be interested in the material he or she is about to present, commenting on the artist as much as on the material; the other is often called "backstory" (about the story) and usually refers to things that the writer needs to know but not necessarily the audience.

I first became aware of preamble in my coffeehouse days at the University of Saskatchewan. A coffeehouse was a euphemism for a gathering and informal concert, invariably in a church basement overseen by some well-meaning youthful clergy type who was trying to get in touch with the "younger generation." I don't recall specifically if there was actual coffee in coffeehouses, but there was certainly no booze — that would have required a license and more trouble than setting up a few tables and chairs with candles on them, then turning out the lights — except for the homemade, lensless tin-can fresnels hanging from the ceiling, pointing at the performance area and bathing it in lurid blue and/or green light. Added to this was smoke from all kinds of cigarettes, not all of them tobacco which the well-meaning youthful clergy pretended not to notice.

Inevitably, some longhaired performer (lad or lass — hair was the first sign of equality between the genders) would mount the stage (a 4x8 sheet of ¾ inch plywood 2 bricks off the floor) and begin to tune his guitar. There seems to have been an unwritten rule that guitars could not be tuned until onstage during which the performer would offer a witty and clever or self-deprecating, and sometimes even thought-provoking ramble introducing the song he was about to perform — if only he could get his guitar in tune. This was often the highlight of the evening for he would eventually abandon the tuning pegs and launch into some mind-numbing dirge as unlike the charming preamble as silk to stone.

Neil Young, whose exceptional talent was always better than his story about the story, introduced one of his compositions with words to this effect: "This song starts off kind of slow before it fizzles out altogether and is guaranteed to bring you down. It's called 'Don't Let It Bring You Down.'" He knew.

This is what I'd say about my stories if I were tuning my guitar:

"Colm" tells a story about a bear on a lake in northern Saskatchewan the essence of which was reported as a news item on CBC radio.

The coyote dragging itself into the woods after having been hit by a car was something I witnessed myself.

The first movement in "Pink Bike Black" is the park — the setting. In my mind's eye it is Buena Vista Park in Old Nutana, Saskatoon. It's a beautiful park and I always wondered who actually built it — it was so obviously done with love.

Couple that observation/interest with the story of Seeger Wheeler, the famous plant breeder of Rosthern, who was involved in selecting and growing the grasses they would eventually use on the golf course being built in the Prince Albert National Park at Waskesui during the 1920s. Mr. Wheeler and an unnamed agrologist from the university were returning on the train from the Park and were so involved in their discussions about what blends of grasses would best suit their purposes that Mr. Wheeler missed his stop at Rosthern and rolled all the way into Saskatoon.

I was once commissioned to write a play about Mr. Wheeler. It became, *Harvest Moon*, produced in Rosthern. Mr. Fogel is based on Mr. Wheeler.

There is a line in the story in which young Hughy describes Mr. Fogel's tools as "all denty and bent." My grandson gave me that line. Perhaps "gave" is the wrong word. Perhaps I stole it from him.

The roots of the story "Hankwoman" came to me years ago when an artist friend told me her mother's dying wish was that she — my friend — ride on a motorcycle. As a rider myself, I was moved by this last request and I eventually wrote this story. When I showed a draft of the story to the person whose experience inspired it, she informed me that I'd got it wrong — that it was her mother who wanted the last ride. And she's not spoken to me since.

"Anna's Flower" is a cut that lay on the editing room floor from a novel I tried to write. The remnants of the failed novel include a novella called *Finding Out Tara* and "Anna's Flower". The events in "Anna's Flower" are autobiographical. Names have been changed of course.

My brother John was/is not "Invisible to Dogs" and bears the scars yet today of where a neighbour's dog bit him on the nose fifty years ago.

"Solo" was the result of an exercise I did with a grade seven class at in La Ronge, Saskatchewan. The object of the task was to adapt a favourite children's story and/or fairy tale and set it in La Ronge. We broke the stories into their "action parts" (a list of what-happened-next) and used them as templates. This took a few weeks and when we were done, we read them aloud in class — mine among them. I'll not say which story I adapted but a hint is the original characters were not human.

"The Big Balloon" in real life was this: a stick with a wheel attached. A cousin made for me. I remember the stick with the wheel attached, but not the cousin who died shortly after he made the toy.

The poet who said "never trust a man with a typewriter between his teeth," was Stanley Cooperman. The "I began my career as a chemist" speech was also his.

The day my daughter was born, my trusty old Volvo B18 did die on our way to the hospital. But her mother and I were picked up by a terrified student returning to Charlottetown, whose small car was filled with her earthly possessions including her cat. "Don't have it yet," she kept pleading to Sharyn who was busy with her Lamaze breathing and avoiding the stick shift. We made it and twenty minutes later, Zoey was born.

The fairy tale in "The Golden Heart" is from my imagination, but the incident of the son discovering his mother's predilection for self-mutilation is real. The specific details of this story are not from within my own family, and will go in confidence with me to the grave.

"Blood and Camping" is a story that began with the title. I liked the implications of blood — as in family — mingled with the possibilities of violence, and the great Canadian penchant for vacationing at a northern lake.

Circa 1970, when my youngest brother and sister were twelve or thirteen, they went camping with my parents somewhere near Beauval where my dad snagged a body in the water with his fishing rod and hauled it in. Although my sister swears this man's hands were tied behind his back, the Saskatoon *StarPhoenix* reported, "no foul play was suspected."

On another occasion, it was my dad who cut his foot needing hospital attention — not a brother. The rest is complete fabrication.

Standing across the street from where I lived as a child (in a tiny house at 123 Avenue T South) was a vacant bungalow surrounded by caraganas and poppies. My grandmother, who spoke only a few words of English, somehow managed to convince me to cross the street, go into that yard, and harvest as many of those poppies as I could. Which I did. I have no idea what she did with them.

However, behind this small house — across the alley on Avenue S — a larger, two-storey house accommodated a trio of women much as they're described in the story "The Witch's Daughters". They were wonderful fodder for a childish imagination and this story is the cumulative speculation on who they were.

The story about the pile of stones and the mystery of its presence was told to me by a woman from Fairy Glen, Saskatchewan. I can't recall her name, but certainly where she came from. It was all too coincidental.

The conceit of the character Kyle's vision wrought by the larvae in his mouth came from what I remember of an oral story Dan Yashinsky once told — only his was about a butterfly flying through a skull.

I was asked to write a story about being poor and since I had pretty good experience at that with my Westside credentials — especially at how normal it is for those who live that way — my attempt was with "Tippy Tango".

I never actually went hungry, but there were spells when the menu my dear mother served was extremely limited. For a time, we lived in a very small suite in my aunt's basement. Tippy was the name of my aunt's dog and, like the dog in the story, was called that for the way its nails clicked upon my aunt's shiny linoleum. I hated that dog. I didn't much care for my aunt either, but her dead son, my cousin, has haunted me throughout my life.

I so remember the very first time I went Christmas shopping. I must have been about the same age as Aiden in "The Diamond Ring". I had about a dollar and a half. For my dad, I bought a roll of black friction tape — so he could tape my hockey stick. What a selfish child I was! This used most of the money I had, but I still had enough to buy my mom a shiny gold corsage for her to pin on her coat. Of course she let on that she was thrilled. My dad, on the other hand, laughed and said thank you. I couldn't figure out what he was laughing at.

I sent a draft of the story "Feeding Piranha" to some friends in Prince Edward Island and, although I had transposed the setting to Saskatchewan, they immediately recognized Milton Acorn as the poet, Pollen. I did in fact approach Milton for a letter of recommendation for my first Canada Council grant many years ago and while the details of the story are pure fiction, the impression of the experience isn't. I got the grant.

Although my dad was decidedly not the Chief Dan George look-alike in "Elk Dog", there was something about his appearance that attracted the romantic eye of an elderly woman from a nearby reserve who openly flirted with him at the local pub in Candle Lake where my parents had a cottage since the early 1970s. My dad never ventured into a bar because he seldom drank — and never beer — but this once he did at the behest of a couple of my brothers and myself. He was extremely upset by the attention this old gal paid him. And we were extremely amused. But it did underscore what he looked like, at least in the eyes of some.

After his death, I discovered his mother's (my grandmother's) name was Annie Poirier, and although I have attempted, I have failed to find any trace of her heritage. It is this slim evidence, and the physical characteristics of some of the MacIntyre descendants, which gave rise to this story.

I also had an uncle who worked in the lumber industry around Carrot River during the 1930s as a cook. The story is that he survived a forest fire at the camp using the method employed by the boys in "Elk Dog".

A friend's mother had a stroke and like the grandfather in this story was bereft of any verbal language except for the words, "Oh! Yes!" and "Oh! No!"

My grandson, Jesse, also gave me the line, "the fire danced inside the smoke." He was about eleven at the time. Again, "gave" might not be the right word.

R.P. MacIntyre's writing has garnered the 2005 Centennial Medal for his contribution to the arts in Saskatchewan, as well as the 1993 Vicky Metcalf Short Story Award for his short story "The Rink", the 1998 Saskatoon Book of the Year Award for his novel *The Crying Jesus* (Thistledown, 1997), and the Canadian Library Association Book of the Year Award for *Takes: Stories for Young Adults* (Thistledown, 1996).